MACHIAVELLIANISM

BOOK TWO OF THE DARK TRIAD TRILOGY

VIOLA TEMPEST

VIOLA TEMPEST PUBLISHING

Machiavellianism
Book Two of The Dark Triad Trilogy

Cover Design by Ann Fleur Art

CONTENTS

Azazel remembered everything. The uprising, the pain of her wings being ripped from her body, and the sinking feeling in her stomach during the fall as she watched the Gates of Heaven grow smaller and smaller the further she fell.

She was once one of the Creator's most beautiful and favored angels who wanted to advance mankind so there wouldn't be a need to interfere like before. God saw this as subordination and ordered that the rebel angels be stripped of their wings so that when He slammed the Gates of Heaven to them, they wouldn't be able to get back in.

Word quickly spread throughout the Kingdom of Heaven

that He was coming for Azazel, her sisters, and the rest of the rebels. There was nowhere they could hide that God couldn't find them. There was no weighing of truth or explanation; God wanted them *gone*. He showed that He wasn't the all-loving God they had once thought He was. His true nature was unforgiving and controlling.

He wanted to keep the humans in the dark, stumbling for answers with only Him as a beacon of hope. With nowhere else to go, they fell to Earth, uncertain of how the humans would react to having divine beings walk amongst them consistently. They should have known that the humans would need to be molded into what the fallen needed them to be in order to survive.

The fallen spread out and concluded that they wanted different things for the humans, and decided to have a millennium-long wager over whose way was the more superior. When the time came, they would shift the world to the path that seemed to fit best for the advancement of humanity.

Azazel didn't see her sisters much unless it was to check in on the progress of each world and compare the progress. She assumed it was because they were embarrassed that their methods weren't working out as well as hers. Azazel had order, luxury, and yearly entertainment that the citizens of her kingdom talked about until the following grand selection.

She lived in paradise and was incredibly confident that *her* way was the only way the world could continue, and humans would have the best hope for survival. Plus, the humans adored her as an earth-bound goddess, and she wouldn't have it any other way.

The humans regularly brought her offerings and renewed their loyalty to satisfy her, hoping she would cancel the yearly Cunning. This event required a member from a selected family to come and fight to the death for riches beyond their wildest dreams. The family would be set up in a luxurious home. Their bank accounts would never be empty.

Over the years, six prominent families had acquired a majority of the wealth in the kingdom. They were able to buy their way out of participating in the Cunning. They were the closest resemblance to friends to Azazel, and took just as much pleasure in watching the event as Azazel did. They had been so successful that it'd been hundreds of years since any of their members had competed. Azazel took so much pleasure in having them close to her. They shared her same beliefs and were always a robust support system for directing the world.

The deaths of the defeated warriors would give Azazel the strength she needed to keep her world balanced. Every year, her subjects would give more extravagant gifts to keep their families intact. Still, Azazel thrived on the chaos that ensued.

After decades of being on Earth, she looked forward to the entertainment of the humans begging for their families. In the weeks leading up to the grand selection, citizens would line up for hours to bring her their most splendid offerings, hoping it would be enough. Her gluttonous nature made her insatiable; her kingdom could give her everything in their homes—even their children—and she would still want more.

And they always found a way to give her *more*. She was never worried about an uprising because she still cared for her kingdom. There was never a food shortage, and everyone had a home. Some were nicer than others, but not one person could complain that they never had enough.

This way of life made it easy for her to start her annual feast. When she first found the area that she took over, it was all lower-class communities. People were miserable, but every person rose in life under Azazel's rule. The citizens became smarter because of the new skills she bestowed on them, wealthier because of the jobs she provided when building the kingdom into what it became, and devious because of the traits that she instilled in them to help them get everything their hearts could ever desire in life.

They realized that the source of their success was Azazel. They were easy to convince.

The Cunning started off with a simple show of who was better at specific archery, swordplay, or basic combat skills. Over the years, things had evolved to become the bloodbath that Azazel loved so dearly. She treated it like it was her birthday or a holiday that everyone should celebrate.

She was never affected by the sorrow many families felt. She knew that death balanced life, and death needed to occur if they wanted to keep their lives the way they were going. While there were rumors that she would eat the souls of the dead, this simply wasn't the case. The soul's essence was automatically attracted to her divinity when they died. It became one with her, giving her the sustenance she eventually needed to continue in the human world. She considered the lost souls safer with her than in Heaven.

As the years passed, Azazel became bored with the display. She eventually decided to create a new theme every year and announce it after the commonwealth funeral to allow potential contestants to train as much as possible before the following grand selection.

The wealthier families had their children training in various combat areas from a young age. Azazel became fond of the younger assassins in her kingdom, and put an age restriction on the selection so that she would never be faced with the sorrow of losing one of her small comrades. By the time they were ready to be chosen, the once young slayers had turned into impressive killing machines. She enjoyed watching them rise in the coliseum until there was only one left.

This had been going on for hundreds of years. Entire generations were lost to appease Azazel, but she was getting to a point where the Cunning was no longer bringing her as much joy. The lost warriors didn't satisfy her as much. The kingdom could feel the air getting heavier as impending doom lingered.

1

Azel looked into her full-length mirror, inspecting herself. The longer she looked, the more obsessed she became. Her long, rich midnight hair flowed around her shoulders. It came down just below her elbows. Her curvaceous body was always clothed in form-fitting gowns made of rich silks in pure white shades. Her jewelry could blind someone if they caught a glimpse of her at the wrong angle midday.

Leaning forward to inspect her expertly-applied makeup, she couldn't help but get lost in her platinum gray eyes and long dark eyelashes. She smiled when she came to her daily realization of how beautiful she was, and how blessed her citizens were to have her as their leader.

She twirled and admired herself even further, loving how the skirt of her dress would slightly fan out and accentuate her curves. She knew how mesmerizing she was. When she faced the mirror again, she applied some gloss to her plump lips and was pleased with her final look for the day.

Walking out of her chamber, the atmosphere in her palace was electric with excitement. It was the morning of the grand selection, and she was looking forward to seeing the entertainment lineup for this year. She smiled at her servants as she passed them, ensuring that they were all doing their duties to keep the palace running smoothly.

Azazel didn't want to start her day by disciplining her staff.

When she noticed one of her butlers moving slower than usual, she went up to him, curious as to what his problem that morning was.

"Cedric?" Azazel smiled sweetly. Cedric bowed profoundly, and she could see that he looked paler than usual. "Are you alright?" Cedric rose from his bow and tried to avoid eye contact with her as he replied. "Just fine, Goddess. I just didn't sleep very well last night."

Azazel gleamed. "Yes, I lose sleep from the excitement on the eve of the grand selection myself, but that isn't an excuse for laziness, now is it?" Her tone dripped with displeasure.

She noticed that he was quick to apologize and claimed he would move quicker going forward.

Cedric excused himself from her presence quickly and carried on, moving faster than before. Azazel stayed and watched him work for a short while until she was satisfied with his speed. She carried on to the Great Hall for her morning tea and breakfast. While she was there, she noticed nervous energy surrounding her, and she couldn't shake it.

Choosing instead to focus on the sweet figs and the comforting tea, wrapping herself in a blanket of reassurance. She knew that the excitement was covering up the fear that the kingdom felt this time of year.

It made her miss Heaven, in the sense that emotions like this weren't felt, so they never interfered with anything that was taking place. Angels generally didn't experience any feelings. They were simply expected to do as they were told without any questions.

It took Azazel and her sisters coming to spend time on Earth to gain any sort of human emotion. It took years for them to feel true happiness and sadness. Azazel hated feeling any kind of negative emotion and manipulated herself to never be obligated to handle any sort of negatively. She repelled any bad feeling, and the person standing closest to her would feel everything that Azazel refused to feel.

As she sat in silence, contemplating the events that were about to unfold, she was curious as to why there was a lingering nervousness in the air. It was almost irritating that they were still nervous after hundreds of years of the grand selection. The Cunning—she thought they would be more than accustomed to it by now. If they really understood how the sacrifice kept their world in balance, they would be celebrating for weeks on end after the final trial instead of mourning the fallen.

Besides, it's not like the souls were lost in Heaven. They were still here, but they had fused with her on a molecular level, and she could still feel their love for her. It was something that she was going to have to address. She needed the energy to be positive and consistent throughout the entire process. It wasn't as fulfilling if they were sad the whole time.

She decided to put a whispered rumor out through her most trusted rumor mongers. She would ensure that the kingdom would understand the weight of this event, and how they all reaped the benefits from the few sacrifices made —and only once a year at that.

Her brow furrowed at the thought of her kingdom thinking the worst of her. She only wanted them to see her as the giving leader she knew she was. If they knew how her hunger provoked her daily, and how hard she had to work to suppress her need for sustenance, they would burst from gratitude for her self-control. She felt her brow furrow at the thought of her urges and sighed, knowing that there was still a short wait before she would feel delighted.

The meals were only for show, so no one would be suspicious of her actual needs. Tapping her fingers on the table, Azazel mulled over the thought of having multiple Cunning events a year, and could feel her mouth salivate at the idea of being full continuously. She decided that maybe this year, it was time to bring the essence of truth into the Cunning, and possibly relieve the mourning families. They should feel honored that their loved ones are a part of her.

Azazel finished her tea and breakfast, and then walked through the halls discreetly, watching her staff as she passed. She knew that there was still time before the selection, but she couldn't wait to see her citizens eager to see if they were chosen.

She went out onto the large balcony at the front of her palace, giving her a bird's eye view of her entire kingdom. Azazel took a deep breath and was instantly refreshed from the morning air. There really *was* something so sacred about this day, and she refused to let there be any underlying negativity.

She decided that she would go down to the selection atrium to inject a bit of divinity to jumpstart the shift, and it would feel right again. She almost ran into her chambermaid, Sarika, and let out an irritated groan as she turned around.

"Sarika! Say something, or make a sound to declare yourself!" Azazel yelled frustratedly.

"I am so incredibly sorry, Goddess. You're right; I should have made myself known." Sarika stumbled through her apology, refusing to look up at Azazel. She bowed low. "I only came to let you know that the grand selection will be taking place soon—"

Azazel interrupted her briskly. "I am aware of the timing, Sarika. I was about to go to the atrium before you held me up with having to explain protocol." Azazel walked past her servant, who rushed behind her to keep up. Azazel was taller than all of the humans she ruled, so keeping up with her long strides required a light run.

"Goddess, if I may," Sarika started and waited for Azazel to acknowledge her. Azazel rolled her eyes and gestured for Sarika to continue. "Goddess, the families are here."

Azazel stopped abruptly. "Why wouldn't you start with that out on the balcony? Do I need to keep explaining to you how to do your job?" Azazel spat at her servant.

Sarika nodded. "They are in the reception hall waiting for you. They haven't been here long."

Azazel seethed. "They shouldn't have been waiting at all, Sarika!" And she quickly turned toward the reception hall, excited to see her most loyal and devoted followers.

As Azazel got closer to them, she could feel herself start to radiate, and it was reflected in all of their faces as they all turned to bow and welcome her.

Azazel scanned the room and opened her arms wide. "Families, welcome!" She beamed at the wealthiest families in her kingdom. The Barem, Ankah, Jones, Li, Thompson, and Berith families all brought forward jewels, extravagant bouquets of flowers, and beautifully-scented body oils.

The fallen angel soaked in the delicious moment and was filled with bliss. She accepted the gifts graciously and blessed each member, ensuring that they would have another year of blessings and happiness.

The families had figured out a loophole in the selection process. Azazel realized this may have not been fair, but she didn't care. The gifts they brought her and the loyalty they showed continuously made up for it all. They all did their part in the kingdom, so that other families could potentially be as successful as them. They taught different combat methods, stayed with mourning family members to ensure they were fine for as long as needed, and always had a hand available to help anyone who needed it. They were the models she was trying to mold the rest of the kingdom into.

The families were always as excited as she was for the great selection and Cunning. Even though they didn't reap the same benefits, the families loved the entertainment.

Making her way through the crowd, she asked eligible members their future plans for marriage. The families only married each other to keep the advantages of their agreement going. Azazel liked to think that it was all because of her; these beautiful families had generations and generations of loved ones, and felt that the very least they could do was shower her with gifts and unwavering loyalty.

Antonio Barem, the current head of the Barem family, stepped forward and dipped low in a bow before stating, "You look absolutely radiant, Goddess."

Azazel couldn't help but be taken by Antonio. He was incredibly handsome with his piercing blue eyes, tanned skin, and the strand of deep blond hair that always found its way to cover one of his eyes. He was always well-dressed and had the best style she had ever seen when it came to men.

He presented her with a velvet case; she smiled and delicately took it from his hands. When she opened it, her breath was taken away. Inside was a strand of the finest diamonds she had ever seen. Antonio came up behind her and pulled the necklace out of the box to indicate that he would adorn her with it. Azazel turned and pulled her hair up to expose her neck so he could take off the necklace that she already had on.

"Ninety of the most precious diamonds ever mined make up this necklace. They reflect the same beautiful colors as the aurora borealis in the light. But they could never compare to your own beauty, Goddess," Antonio whispered into her ear as he connected it.

He let his fingertips lightly brush against her exposed shoulders, and Azazel shivered ever so slightly in pleasure. She couldn't understand this hold that Antonio had on her. It was otherworldly.

She turned to him and cupped his face softly. "You have outdone yourself yet again, Antonio. It's beautiful." And she placed her hand on the necklace.

This gift felt different from the hundreds he had presented to her over the past years. Members of the other families all brought up different offerings. As pleased as she was with everything, Azazel couldn't help but continue to glance at Antonio, who watched her intently. His eyes filled with a look that she couldn't put her finger on.

After the offerings had been given, and Azazel was pleased, she motioned toward the exit

"Shall we?" she asked before turning to lead her courtiers out of the grand hall.

As they walked out of the palace gates together, Azazel couldn't help but notice the kingdom's beauty. Garlands of flowers were strung between street lamps, and the bakeries were busy producing sweet-smelling treats to be handed out. Azazel felt at peace and wanted to enjoy every moment leading up to the Cunning.

Children ran up to the group with flowers to offer to Azazel; she couldn't help but be swept up by the sweetness of every human she came into contact with. The entire group had multiple bouquets in their hands when they got to the atrium. When they stepped into the main entrance of the atrium, they all turned to walk to the small altar located to the left of the main arena. This was where citizens would come daily to leave offerings, and the entire shrine was engulfed with tokens of affection. Azazel's heart always swelled when she saw the shrine. It was a visual confirmation of her people's love, and it showed what they were capable of when it came to the grandness of their offerings.

The families all laid the flowers in front of the shrine, filling the room with a sweet floral scent. Azazel was in pure bliss, watching the scene in front of her. The families gathered in front of the shrine to say a prayer, thanking the Universe for bringing them their goddess.

Azazel was grateful for her courtiers. She never knew this kind of appreciation when she was in Heaven. She was solely expected to keep giving more and more of herself with every task that God gave her. Ask no questions, and get it done as quickly as possible. Azazel took a moment to enjoy the offerings before the atrium steward came to get them. The time had finally come for the grand selection. All of the families went to the spectator's box built at the highest point of the atrium. At the same time, Azazel made her way to the stage located in the middle of the arena.

2

Azazel walked onto the stage, and the audience broke out into thunderous applause. She looked around the entire arena, loving every second of the outpouring of affection. People were jumping up and down, trying to get her attention. Azazel couldn't help but smile widely; she wanted them to enjoy the excitement for as long as possible before many were sent into a downward spiral. After a short time passed, Azazel turned to the table and grabbed the list and microphone. She turned toward the crowd and motioned for them to quiet down.

The silence that came afterward was deafening in its own right. Everyone waited and collectively held their breath, and

Azazel could feel the tension of the kingdom, waiting to see what she would say. She scanned the room one last time.

When she looked up, she saw Antonio's face, and something in his face brought her overwhelming comfort. She cleared her throat, thanked everyone for participating, and thanked them for their continued love and devotion. This caused the crowd to erupt in a booming response, which she fully expected.

What she didn't expect, however, was after the first name was read, the wailing of the combatant's mother took over the entire atrium. Sounding like a wounded animal, it was guttural, primal, and filled with deep pain. Azazel realized at once after looking back at the last name that the woman's entire family had been lost to the Cunning. Her son would be the final member, and she'd be left all alone. Azazel hated seeing this happen, even after all this time.

Azazel waited for her crying to cease and continued until all hundred names were called. The combatants were brought down to the stage so Azazel could get a better look at all of them, and was pleased to see that they were primed to fight and were in the best shape possible. Azazel didn't think this selection could get any better, because they were all at the top of their rankings for different combat methods.

The steward came to give her a scroll with the following year's theme. She smiled when she read *gladiators*, which meant lions would be brought back into the kingdom. Azazel smiled, already looking forward to next year. The steward bowed, pleased to see how excited his goddess was. He took the scroll from her and left the stage; it was time to go through the Cunning's series of events. Azazel turned back to the crowd and put her hands up to indicate that it was time to listen.

Once the crowd had gone quiet, Azazel beamed as she announced that for the theme this year, Ultimate Warrior, the combatants would be put into the harshest conditions that would change day to day to test their survival skills. She also made it known that there would be a base camp in the middle of the arena with essential tools, a backpack for each warrior that contained everything they would need to set up their own camp, clothing for every season, and limited food packets. This year was going to be intense as they celebrated the two thousandth anniversary of the Cunning. She allowed the community to sponsor the combatants for the first time while they completed their two-week initiation training. The more money they raised, the better-quality gear they acquired at base camp. Azazel was keen to see the ways the warriors got creative.

After announcing the series of events and explaining the differences this year, she established her expectations for surprises at every turn, putting immense pressure on the game masters. When Azazel got bored, she took things into her own hands. She would hold the people responsible for her boredom accountable. They often weren't seen again.

Turning to head away from the crowd and warriors, her part was done for the day. Now it was time for the public offerings, her favorite part of the event. She made her way out of the atrium and toward the kingdom's center. There was a grand throne made out of marble on the place where she landed when she fell from Heaven; it was one of the most sacred places in the entire kingdom.

Azazel walked up to her throne. She sat down and positioned herself, sitting straight up and making sure she had her dress fanned out around her while waiting for the first offering. Antonio came to the platform and stood beside the throne silently for quite a while before breaking the silence after the latest offering.

"Are you pleased so far, Goddess?" He scanned the long

line of citizens all waiting patiently and murmuring amongst themselves, comparing their gifts.

Azazel smiled up at him and reached out to grab his forearm as she said, "Oh, yes, very much so."

She motioned to the mound of gifts opposite of them. She couldn't wait to have everything in her palace. Azazel loved to fill her home with beautiful things and enjoyed that she could change her decor every year.

Antonio nodded encouragingly. "Yes, the kingdom has had a very successful year. It's truly our honor to do this for you, Goddess." He bowed to her, and Azazel felt giddy.

"Antonio, do you really think there is any need for the formality at this point?" she purred. Antonio looked up at her. She batted her eyelashes sweetly at him.

The gaze they shared was charged, and Azazel caught her breath in her throat, suddenly nervous. The next citizen then came up and cleared their throat, breaking the tension. Azazel broke eye contact first and accepted the gift, thanking the citizen. When she looked back, Antonio was still staring at her, taking in every detail of her face. Azazel felt her face flush and turned back to her adoring admirers. Her mind was racing with the flashbacks of the intense moments with Antonio.

She didn't understand where this was coming from. He had been her loyal subject for so long at this point, and she found herself wondering why she felt so nervous around him all of a sudden. She pushed her personal problems aside and focused on the offerings again; she smiled and began basking in the love that her kingdom was so willing to give.

After the last person had come to give their gift, Azazel sat for a moment and looked around the clearing. She felt like she had been there for weeks, and her face was starting to feel sore from the constant smiling. She was looking forward to sleeping for a long time after the Cunning.

Azazel stood up and figured it was time to check in on the combatants, and so she headed toward the training arena. Looking into the sky and noticing the sun setting, she suddenly remembered that the warriors would be getting ready to eat, and she smiled to herself, knowing that the warriors would be eating like royalty for their training session. Azazel always ensured that the best and most nutritious meals were prepared for them. Hence, they felt like they were cared for up until the end. She also noticed that the more satisfied their bodies were, the more satisfying their souls were when she absorbed them.

The angel let herself into the side door that led through a secret tunnel, and eventually, a room secretly hidden by a one-way mirrored glass. She was pleased to see that the warriors were still training so she wouldn't have to come back. She faced two combatants engaging in martial arts when she looked out the window. She recognized the boy as the first name she called; Azazel was pleasantly surprised when she saw him flip his opponent onto his back and win the match. She watched a while longer to witness him win every match that he was placed in. He had something to fight for, which meant he was a threat.

Pleased with what she saw, Azazel walked out of the arena, thrilled with the selection of combatants this year. The atrium steward waited for her when she came out of the building.

"Ah, Goddess, excellent. I was hoping you'd be here," he said as he bowed low.

"My curiosity got the better of me," Azazel replied shortly. "I was just about to head back to my abode."

The steward stood up. "Yes, of course, Goddess. I just wanted to go over the schedule for tomorrow."

Azazel stopped, already exhausted from the day she just had. She let out a sigh. "Steward, I am going to leave everything up to you. I am washing my hands of this responsibility. Do not bore me." Then she walked past him, leaving him open-mouthed and anxious.

Azazel loved walking through her kingdom by herself. She was never worried about people coming up to her. They feared and respected her so much that they all kept their distance unless it was a holy day. And she *loved* how the kingdom was decorated this year. Her people seemed to find new and innovative ways to make the kingdom look stunning every year, and they never repeated any styles from previous years.

She was always so impressed with her citizens and how they showed their love for her. She was overwhelmed with gratitude for her people during her entire walk back to the palace. As she got ready, she thought about the upcoming weeks and the festivities that were about to take place. When she laid her head down on her pillow, Antonio's face was swimming around in her mind. His smile was the last thing she remembered before sleep overtook her.

3

Azazel opened her eyes the following day and was instantly excited. In a grand parade, she'd get to show off her combatants to the kingdom today. Each contestant would be dressed in the most luxurious materials and proudly display their family crest, honoring their ancestors and living family members. Azazel always enjoyed the pride she felt in those moments.

She stretched her arms wide, cracking her spine slightly and running her hand over her back. She felt the two scarred spots on her shoulder blades where her wings once were. Refusing to feel sad for her loss, she focused on her combatants and their achievements instead.

Azazel quickly jumped out of bed and ran to her ample walk-in closet to pick the perfect outfit. She settled on a deep red bandage dress that hugged her curves and ended just above her knee. She also selected a pair of platform strappy sandals and picked out the necklace that Antonio had presented her with the previous day. Picking up the delicate necklace, she couldn't help but get lost in the beauty of the diamonds. Azazel wondered if there were other underlying motives behind the beauty of the offering but quickly pushed that out of her head. She was his goddess, and it was solely a gift of devotion. She decided that that's the only motive he had and finished her swooning over a mere human.

She did have to admit that the necklace elevated her look. It truly made her sparkle like the brightest star in the sky. She decided that she didn't need any other jewels and went into her beauty room, where the makeup artist was waiting to apply her makeup and style her hair for the day. She sat and enjoyed being pampered, mulling over the day's possibilities ahead of her.

Once the servant stepped back, saying she was finished, Azazel got up to inspect her face in the mirror. She was absolutely pleased with the dark and mysterious look that made her eyes pop out and the pouty red lips that she was so famous for shine. She couldn't help but smile and comment, "My hair has a certain luster to it today."

The servant mumbled, "Yes, Goddess, you are stunning," without making eye contact.

After a sufficient amount of gushing over herself in the mirror, Azazel left the beauty room and walked toward the dining room. She had a craving for sweet fruits and tea this morning. As she took her seat, the staff came out with a wave of plates and platters filled with different types of food. They set them all in front of her to pick and choose however she wanted.

Taking a ripe strawberry and savoring the sweet juice—even though she never experienced much taste from earthly food—she enjoyed the texture of the fruit in her mouth. She then grabbed the tiny teacup beside her and took a sip, and the warmth and comfort from the chai tea washed over her. Nothing could go wrong today, especially not when the tea was made this perfect.

Once she was satisfied with her grazing and the tea was finished, Azazel got up from the elegant table and walked toward the palace's front entrance. She almost collided with the rushing atrium steward, who dropped to his knees when he saw her.

"Goddess, we are waiting for you to start the proceedings." He didn't look up at her.

Azazel was agitated by his statement. Her face contorted into a look of disgust. "Are you sure that's how you want to greet me this morning, Steward?" Looking down at him, she couldn't help but notice his receding hairline, disheveled and wrinkled clothing. He smelled like he had just walked out of the bar. She wondered if maybe she had put too much faith into the steward.

Without looking up, he replied, "Goddess, the people of the kingdom have been lining the streets since dawn, waiting for you to grace them with your presence."

Azazel sucked air in through her teeth. "Not much better, Steward."

He looked up to reply. "Tom, Goddess, my name is Tom—"

Azazel cut him off sharply. "I don't care what your name is, Steward." And she walked past him through the heavy, elaborate double doors.

As she stepped outside, her loyal courtiers were waiting for her in the divine gardens that surrounded the palace. As she got closer to the group, an elderly woman from the

Thompson family—with silver hair pulled up into a tight bun—stepped forward, curtsied, and asked in a concerned tone. "Goddess, are you alright? You… you look displeased."

Azazel let out a long sigh before replying, "Yes, Catherine, thank you. Dealing with saboteurs so early in the morning is enough to ruin anyone's day."

Catherine looked back at her family, and then back to Azazel. "Saboteurs, Goddess?"

Azazel nodded. "I consider unruly behavior to be saboteur behavior, don't you?"

Catherine didn't say anything, but she nodded in agreement and turned back to her family. This wasn't how Azazel had intended for the day to go. Now she would have to find a replacement for the atrium steward at the very beginning of the festivities. Azazel's whole morning had turned sour.

She tried not to let it seep into her mood as she made her way through the crowd and faced them all, holding her arms open and welcoming them. Putting on a smile and allowing herself to relax again, she turned and led the crowd out of the gardens and down the main street to where her marble throne sat. Azazel took her place, seated in the middle of the kingdom. She took a deep breath and let herself feel the pure divine energy from the holiest site in the entire kingdom.

Taking in several deep breaths to cleanse herself of the negative feelings that she was forced to feel earlier, she opened her eyes and motioned with her hand to start the parade. Almost instantly, a fanfare could be heard a distance away. As the music grew closer, Azazel was still trying to calm her annoyance from the encounter with the steward earlier.

Almost as if he could sense that she was thinking of him, the foul-smelling steward showed up by her side. He had his hands clasped in front of his waist, watching the square in front of him. Azazel could sense that he was about to say something, so she held up one finger to him.

"Your services will no longer be needed. Your termination is effective immediately. You are to come to my chamber tonight when the moon is at the highest point in the sky." She looked at him and could see that his face turned quite pale. She raised her eyebrows. "I said, you can go," she said with pure venom.

He bowed his head and walked away from her. Once he was gone, a large smile came across Azazel's face, and she felt relaxed, just in time. The band came around the corner, and her spirit was instantly lifted as she heard that the band had written a new melody in her honor. Leaning back and closing her eyes so she could enjoy the music, she felt herself slip into pure bliss.

When she opened her eyes again, the first combatants followed the band. She smiled warmly to welcome them. The line of fighters walked in a single file, all wearing tailored clothing in black. She admired everyone and noticed that they'd look at her, make eye contact, and then continue their march. Usually, several would break eye contact out of nervousness, but no one in this group seemed to show any emotion. She liked their confidence and could tell that this year's Cunning would be a satisfying experience in every sense.

The families followed the combatants and announced who they were sponsoring so far. Other wealthy families came forward to claim their own sponsors until every combatant was taken.

Even though she tried to never feel human emotions, Azazel couldn't help but feel relief for the fighters. Knowing fully well that they'd still have their needs met in a stressful situation that would make or break them. Azazel was giddy, thinking about the possibilities of how they were going to really keep her guessing.

Once she approved the pairings, she stood up. She announced that she would need Antonio, his brother, Jacob, and two strong family members from the Li family to stay behind. Thankfully, the selection was made quickly, and she was pleased to see two of the biggest Li family members come forward. Azazel announced that the kingdom was dismissed, and they were to refrain from coming out of their homes until the following day. She heard the confused mumbling through the crowd but paid it no mind.

After the kingdom had gone back into their homes, and Azazel was convinced that they were finally alone, she pulled the four men closer to her and told them that she was looking for the former atrium steward. She wanted him brought to her chamber, indicating that they didn't need to be gentle with him, either. The men all took off in different directions. Feeling satisfied, Azazel slowly walked home, excited to have a snack before the main course. Her mouth watered in excitement. She was eager to forget that he'd ever existed.

When Azazel returned to the palace, she walked into the dining room and grabbed the teapot and cup, and put them on a large platter filled with fruit, thinking it would be an excellent way to end her meal. She walked past the same servants whom she had chastised that morning and smiled at everyone as she passed them. Pleased with their newfound work ethic, she finally made it to her chamber, where she found several servants turning her bed down. She left the door open as she stepped aside.

"Out, now. I don't want to be disturbed until Antonio, his brother, and the Li brothers come."

The chambermaids curtsied and replied, "Yes, Goddess," in unison. Azazel was borderline impressed with their timing.

When they left, she locked the door and decided that she needed to slip into something a bit more appropriate. Walking into her closet, she went to find a light pink silk kimono. She pulled it out and thought it was perfect. She undressed and put her clothes off to the side for the following day's laundry gathering. Looking at herself in the mirror, she was incredibly pleased with how incredible her body looked, even in a robe. Azazel smiled and pulled it tighter, really accentuating her waist. She wanted to give Antonio something to think about when he left.

Just as she walked out of her closet, she heard a light knock on the door. Azazel went over and unlocked the entrance to the Li brothers looking disheveled. Antonio holding the scruff of the disgraced steward's clothing, she stepped aside and allowed them into her chamber. Antonio forced the scrawny man through the door behind the brutish brothers. When the five of them all came in, Azazel looked concerned.

"Antonio, where is your brother?" Hoping no harm came to him, Antonio quickly put her concern to rest.

"Jacob ripped his clothing in the chase. Goddess, he's alright. He just ran home to change so you wouldn't be offended by his appearance." The Li brothers looked at each other, and then looked at Antonio as if they were insulted.

Azazel quickly interjected. "I am so grateful to all of you for putting in the work to bring him to me." She smiled and looked at each man, lingering on Antonio, whose eyes were dark with an emotion she could only label as lust.

She told the Li brothers to let the steward go, who fell to the floor between them all. He looked up at Azazel.

"Please, Goddess, I didn't mean to offend you."

This caused Azazel to scoff. "Offend me? Your lack of drive offended me, your stench offended me, and your entire being offended me." The man started to whimper and repeatedly apologized. Azazel looked up to the men behind him. "You are all dismissed; thank you again."

Antonio paused while the other men left. "Are you sure you don't want anything else, Goddess?"

As he finished his sentence, Jacob ran down the hall to where they were standing. Azazel stepped over the pathetic pile on the floor and rested her hand on his arm.

"Yes, Antonio, we are going to be just fine here. Thank you again for your dedication." She guided him gently out of her room. Before Jacob could say anything, Azazel closed the door after giving him a small smile.

Azazel turned back to the man on her floor; she stepped over him again and sat on a chair that was opposite him. He was saying a prayer, and this irked Azazel. "Your God cannot help you here!" She sneered at him, causing him to start sniveling louder.

"Please, Goddess, please forgive me. I am so sorry with all of my soul!" He moved closer to her and started kissing her bare feet. This caused her to recoil in disgust and shove him back violently with her foot.

"Don't touch me, you stupid little gremlin!" The steward curled up into a ball on the floor, slightly rocking back and forth as he started to have a mental breakdown.

Azazel calmly poured a cup of tea and sipped it while he went through a rollercoaster of emotions at her feet. When she finished her tea and felt like she had calmed down significantly, she asked him softly, "What do you think happens to the combatants after they die?" She was curious to see if the rumors in the kingdom had changed at all.

The man stopped his pathetic moaning and looked up at

her, wiping his nose. He asked, "They are buried, aren't they?"

Azazel shook her head. "No, what do you think happens to their souls after they die?"

He thought about it for a few moments. "Well, Goddess, our souls are no longer allowed into Heaven after your banishment… so I would think the souls are either stuck in Purgatory or in Hell." While the answer impressed her, it didn't feed her gossip inquiry.

Azazel nodded. "What if I told you that the souls never really leave?"

This caused the steward to look up at her in confusion. "Leave, Goddess? How would they stay?" He started, looking around as if dead people would be coming out of her closet or from under her bed.

Azazel took in a breath. "The souls never leave."

The steward started to panic a little as Azazel stood up. "Goddess, what do you mean, the souls never leave?"

He began to back away as she got closer. She shushed him and crouched down on top of him. He groaned under her divine weight, crushed by her.

Azazel then leaned forward, so that their lips were almost touching when she whispered, "They are safer with me than in Heaven." The steward's eyes grew wide with fear when he realized what she's talking about.

Azazel kissed his lips and got off of him to go to her bedside table, and she quickly came back with a long black dagger. The steward started to scramble away from her, and she stepped on his ankle, instantly breaking it and causing him to scream out in pain. Quickly straddling him, she came close and brought the blade to his throat.

"You had a simple job, Steward, to keep me entertained. You couldn't even do that. You were supposed to be a representation of me in the atrium. The only things you represented were alcoholism and squalor. I'm doing the kingdom a service." Azazel pulled the blade across the thin skin on his neck, causing blood to flow out quickly. She then smiled as she leaned down to the dying man to say, "Let go."

He fought for his pathetic life longer than she'd expected, and then she adjusted herself so she was directly over top of his lungs, restricting his airflow even further. She looked down at him and whispered, "Normally, I would give you something to take the edge off so this could be a beautiful bonding moment between us, but I'd much rather watch you struggle."

The man made a grunting sound and was severely strained. His breaths grew shallow and his eyes grew wider, realizing that he was dying. Azazel eagerly waited until the moment finally came, where a small blinding white orb started to float out of his mouth. She bent down and inhaled the orb into her mouth, throwing her head back as the soul instantly revived her. Her hair looked luscious and healthy, skin pink and plump, and any age marks that had started to show were immediately gone. Azazel sat on the body until she felt fully rejuvenated.

Standing up, she went over to her door and yelled for clean-up. Without giving it a second thought, she went into her bathroom to draw a hot bath and no longer wanted to look at a dead body. As she disrobed, she fell in love with herself, surprised that such a skeevy human being could give her these kinds of results.

5

Azel drew a hot bath and dropped in some lavender oils. As the floral smell wafted up into her nose, she could hear some thumping around in her main chamber but decided not to pay it any mind. She would let the clean-up crew do their thing uninterrupted while she soaked away her worries.

Dropping her robe around her ankles, she inspected her body again. Even though her body looked impeccable before she absorbed the whiny little man, her skin now looked pink and plump. She noticed that her backside was lifted more and her legs looked more tone.

Happy with the results, she stepped into the tub and sighed as she sat down in the hot sweet-smelling water. She felt euphoric as she had flashbacks of the absorption and the look of fear in the steward's eyes when he realized he was going to die. The whole situation was so delicious, and she was looking forward to doing it again very soon.

When she thought about the steward's squirming, she grew irritated. Usually, she would have given her victim her golden touch to be more compliant to what she wanted them to do, like little puppets whose strings were wrapped around her fingers. And even though the kingdom was already filled with puppets, and as hard as she tried to keep them at ease initially, they seemed to freak out when they realized what was about to occur.

Azazel mentally transported back to the time when she had first founded the kingdom. Her people respected her divinity. She was their only leader, one who aged and wasn't very attractive, one who was still healing her internal wounds from being rejected by the highest being. She realized that she needed a heavier hand to guide the humans to do what she wanted.

Azazel decided that the humans needed to be strong-armed into doing what she wanted. She concocted a unique drug and laced the kingdom's water supply with it. That's what made it so easy for her to take over the kingdom and mold it however she saw fit without interference from people who didn't want to listen to her new rules. Azazel smiled at the memory of when the full effect took place, and she held the first ever Cunning.

She had been on Earth for a decade at that point, looking for ways to keep herself satisfied and eating everything in sight. Yet her hair kept falling out, and her skin was wrinkling. She came to her absorption solution completely by accident when she came across a dying homeless man, knelt down to comfort him as he sputtered his last breath, and his soul orb came floating out of his mouth—and something inside of her told her to ingest it. When she did, the rejuvenation process happened instantly, and she knew then that this was the way she would be able to survive on Earth.

When she got back home, she demanded that every book from the library on narcotics and their effects be brought to her chamber immediately. Azazel consumed stack after stack of books and decided to mix a combination of psychedelics together. When she lost a few of her servants in the process trying to get the dosage right, it was a good thing they were enough to tie her hunger over, but this was also when the hunger started to take full effect. When Azazel finally got the dosage right, she realized that it didn't affect the victims long enough, and they would try to fight her off still.

Later that night, she concluded that she would use the very last of her angelic powers to make her touch have the same effect as the drug whenever she wanted it to. Tonight, she just wanted to make the pathetic steward suffer with his fear as he died. She thought his soul would taste foul; she wanted the fear to sweeten it a little for her. Azazel smiled at how dark her mind was as she leaned back and let her hair fully submerge into the water, which welcomed her like an old friend.

When she brought her head above the water again, she didn't hear anyone shuffling around in her chamber anymore and decided that it was a good time to get out of the bath. She grabbed a plush white towel and wrapped her robe around herself. This time when she went over to the mirror, she grabbed a brush and ran it through her long hair and applied thick lotion all over her body to ensure she remained as supple as ever.

Feeling thoroughly moisturized, she turned and walked over to her closet and pulled out a light pink nightgown with black lace around the hem. For the final time, she stood in front of her floor-length mirror. The nightgown hugged her body so well. It was almost a shame that she was the only one who would ever see it. She smiled when the name Antonio flashed across her mind. Azazel was sure that if she called him, he would come running.

She got changed and eagerly walked into her bedroom. When she saw her luxurious four-poster bed, she stopped. Everything she had done until this point had been worth it; her people had never been happier, and more importantly, *she* had never been happier. Azazel climbed onto her bed and sank into the plush and thick pillows. She felt herself fully relaxed for the first time in a long time. It's incredible what one sacrifice could do for an earth-bound goddess. Azazel smiled to herself. She loved the dark places that her mind went to tonight. Maybe she needed to take it there more often.

Azazel couldn't help but think of all of the combatants she had absorbed throughout the years and the strength that they had given her. She felt her skin start to vibrate, and she smiled wider, knowing that on some level, they could still feel her gratitude radiating for them. Curious as to how the newest recruits would affect her, Azazel couldn't sleep. She spent a good part of the night wondering how each one would taste and make her feel. When she thought of the boy whose name she called first, she felt a pit in her stomach. She wasn't sure why he was different, but she sensed that he had quite a few tricks up his sleeve in order to go as far as possible.

She sat in silence and realized that sleep wouldn't relieve her anytime soon. Azazel started thinking about Antonio. She felt her face flush in the dark at the thought of his fingers lingering on her back when he placed his necklace on her, and how her body reacted to him. Azazel considered that maybe she should suggest that he become her consort. Smiling at the thought of handsome Antonio Barem in her bed, she decided that she would offer it in the morning. She was tired of the tension between them and wanted to finally act on it.

6

When she opened her eyes the following day, she was extremely happy. It was a full training day for the combatants, and she would be spending a majority of the day in the training center with the sponsors and families. As she sat up, the night before came rushing into her head, and she couldn't help but feel even happier.

Jumping out of bed and heading right into her closet, she picked out a long nude-colored gown with delicate diamond beading that accentuated her chest and hips. She would be proposing the consort idea to Antonio today, and she didn't want to leave anything to his imagination.

When she put the gown on, the diamonds accentuated her curves, and she knew that Antonio wouldn't have a real choice in the matter. She didn't want to use her touch on him. Azazel wanted her body to entice him enough so that he'd come all on his own. Grabbing a pair of black strappy platforms and the necklace from Antonio, she went into her makeup room, telling her chambermaids that she wanted her makeup to look sultry and her hair ethereal. She was pleased with how much her eyes stood out and how pouty her lips looked when she was done. Her hair was loosely curled and looked like a halo around her when she stood in front of the window light to get a better look in the mirror. It was perfect, and she knew it was the *perfect* look to propose this idea to Antonio.

Azazel then dismissed the maid and walked out of the room toward the dining hall. She wasn't hungry this morning, but she knew she had to keep up with appearances. She grabbed a few slices of the cut apple and seemed to inhale her chai tea before tossing the cup back onto the table, shattering it. Azazel lifted her brows at her carelessness and called for a servant to come and clean it up. When they walked into the room, she left before they could bow to her. Azazel only had one thing on her mind when she walked out of the palace with the apple slices, and she wasn't paying attention to anything else around her. She just wanted to see Antonio's face.

As she walked closer to the training arena, she felt herself getting nervous. She knew that Antonio wouldn't necessarily reject her, but he might have some worries about lying down with a goddess. She smiled, knowing that she would teach him how to be with her in every meaning of the word.

Walking into the arena's front door, she was pleased to see the combatants already training extensively. It looked like they had already been at it for hours. Everyone was saturated with sweat. When the instructor noticed her entering the arena, he halted the training and had everyone bow to her as she passed them to her chair on a platform high above them.

She seemed to have just sat down when Antonio showed up at her side. "Good morning, Goddess, you look absolutely radiant this morning. If you're not careful, the sun will become jealous."

Azazel looked into his eyes. "It would have done me a lot of good to hear that first thing this morning."

It was Antonio's turn to blush as he inquired, "Did you require me to stay later last night, Goddess? Was there a problem with the steward?" His face then distorted into a look of worry.

Azazel was touched by his concern and reassuringly said, "Oh, Antonio, you're so sweet. No, the steward is now only a figment of our imagination. Please don't give him another thought." She smiled at him and touched his arm lightly.

Antonio crouched down to her level. "Goddess, please tell me what you mean."

His eyes pleaded with hers, and Azazel came closer to him. "I've been thinking about the possibility of taking a consort," she said quietly, which made Antonio's eyes grow wide, intrigued.

"Really, Goddess? And who would the lucky man be? Or were you considering having some sort of tournament for your hand?"

Azazel could see the gears turning in his head as she asked, "Would you compete, Antonio? If there were going to be a tournament?"

Antonio's face suddenly turned serious when he replied, "There would be no need for a tournament when I know I would win; no need to embarrass every man in the kingdom."

Azazel smiled at him. "I was hoping you'd say something like that. Come to my chamber for dinner tonight. We can discuss it further."

Antonio stood up and bowed. "Yes, Goddess. I'll be counting down the minutes." He backed away from her so that she could focus solely on her combatants, who had just started working with different types of weapons.

Azazel couldn't help but feel pure excitement. She loved watching the humans fight with pointy objects. Watching them dance around each other, she appreciated the beauty of combat sports and knew it was the most honorable way to die in this world.

She watched as a medium-built blonde girl kicked another girl in the chest and launched her several feet away from their sparring. The blonde girl then walked over to her victim with katanas in her hands. It was clear to everyone watching that she was out for blood and had to be pulled out of the fighting arena.

Azazel smiled at the feistiness of her newest playthings. The staff went to help up the injured girl, and it seemed like she only had the wind knocked out of her, no severe damage. Azazel could see the fire ignited in her eyes and knew she was ready for another round.

Scanning the arena, Azazel could see many combatants showing the same intensity, and she definitely wanted to meet them. She may want to even take a gamble on a couple. She thought about the steward and how he affected her when she absorbed him, and she grew increasingly excited for what these delicious morsels would do for her.

She let herself out of the spectator's box and made her way down the flight of stairs until she was stepping into the arena. The warriors stopped sparring and formed a single line, standing straight and focused when a high-pitched whistle blew. Azazel walked down the line, and each combatant introduced themselves and told her their top three combat skills. By the time she reached the end of the line, Azazel had the largest grin. She couldn't help but appreciate what a great day it was.

The trainer blew the whistle again, and they dispersed, pairing up again and sparring once more. Azazel was impressed with the precise and calculated movements of each pairing. The trainer told her some random facts about the group; however, Azazel wasn't listening. She watched combatant number one, Thomas O'Donoghue, and she was surprised that he moved swiftly and efficiently for such a large young man. She knew that if she was going to bet on anyone, it would be him, and decided that she would throw some money in to sponsor him.

Thanking the trainer for introducing her to them and complimenting him on his progress with his charges, Azazel left the arena after a few more minutes, looking forward to the Cunning even more than she did earlier this morning. As she walked through the kingdom, she passed many residents who bowed low and waited for her to cross. Azazel walked with her head held high and had an aura about her that was intoxicating and filled the humans she watched over with a euphoric feeling whenever she was near them. She was so happy to see them today and could feel the excitement in the air over the upcoming festivities. They had no idea about the level of entertainment that they were in for.

Azazel made her way through the streets and back into her palace to get ready for her dinner with Antonio. She was in the mood for pasta, and decided she would let the chef know that that's what she would like prepared for dinner tonight and brought directly to her chamber. As she walked into the kitchen, she could see the chef already putting a sheet of homemade pasta through a pasta maker and was pleasantly surprised. The chef noticed her and tried to bow, but Azazel told him to stop and show his gratitude through his meals instead. She left the kitchen in very high spirits and headed to her chamber to get herself ready.

When she arrived, she dismissed the chambermaids for the night but asked them to fetch the makeup artist before they clocked out.

The servants all bowed and replied in unison, "Yes, Goddess."

Azazel smiled and asked, "You guys practice that?"

They responded "no," again in unison and looked at each other.

Azazel chuckled. "Alright, off with you."

The maids dipped in a quick curtsy and left the room. Azazel went into her bathroom and started the water. This time, she dropped in vanilla and patchouli, and secured her long hair up on the top of her head with two hair sticks. She got undressed and placed her clothes off to the side. As she stepped into the water, she surrendered to the stirring possibility that was quickly approaching. Smiling at the thought of Antonio once again, she heard the door open and the makeup artist hollering for her.

Azazel replied that she'd be out shortly and washed herself. She cupped water over her shoulders to rinse the rich lather off, leaving behind the vanilla and patchouli scent, taking her intoxication level to another world. Azazel knew Antonio wouldn't be able to resist, but she wanted him to enjoy it, too.

When she felt clean and smelled like a dream, she pulled herself out of the tub and dried off before wrapping herself in her plush robe. Azazel walked out to her room to see her makeup artist, Monica, laying out all of her supplies and had the curler already heating up. Monica dropped down in a curtsy, and Azazel thanked her for coming so quickly.

Monica then slapped the chair and asked what they were doing.

Azazel didn't know where to start with her outfit. Still, she told Monica that she was getting ready for a private dinner with someone extraordinary. She planned on dismissing all of her staff for the evening, keeping it as hush as possible until they were ready to announce the news. Monica listened and beamed at her leader. She took the hair sticks out of Azazel's hair, looked at her in the mirror, and said, "Let's begin."

7

Azazel let herself fall into the hypnotic feeling and enjoyed Monica doing her hair. She closed her eyes and allowed Monica to have free reign. Azazel had never been disappointed with Monica's vision when it came to her look. The makeup artist had worked for Azazel for over ten years, and was a genius when it came to color theory and making sure Azazel's eyes were the most enticing part of her image.

Losing track of time, Azazel was almost asleep when Monica finally interrupted the silence. "Goddess, you're ready," and Azazel opened her eyes. She gasped.

Monica had made her hair wavy and free flowing,

framing her face and coming around her shoulders while her eyes were lined in black and smoked out with a single glitter start in the inner corner. And the nude lip color was absolute perfection! Azazel stood up and gushed over her appearance, commending Monica on her skills and then telling her that she was dismissed for the evening, and to come in later than usual the next day. Monica bowed low and thanked Azazel for allowing her to apply her makeup and waited for Azazel to leave the room before she started to clean up the tools that she had laid out.

Turning her attention to what she was going to wear, Azazel made her way toward her closet and walked down the side with her most treasured gowns, several in every color and every design made just for her. Azazel had a difficult time picking which one she wanted to grace her body with but eventually settled on a simple black strapless dress that came down to her thigh, and gold pumps with an ankle strap that looked like a serpent. Once she put the shoes on and wrapped the serpent around her ankle, Azazel stood up and inspected herself in the mirror, extremely pleased with the reflection looking back at her.

When she left the closet, she was pleased to see that Monica had left, and a small table with two chairs had been brought in, set with candles and everything needed for the intimate dinner. Azazel went to a cabinet near her closet door and brought out several sets of candles, and she placed them lit all around the room, giving it an even cozier atmosphere. She shut off the lights and looked around her bedroom, admiring how beautiful it was.

Soon after she'd set up the candles, she heard a soft knock on the door. Azazel took a deep breath before she opened the door to Antonio, who was dressed in a pair of black dress pants and a deep navy button-down that had the first two buttons undone. His hair fell deliciously over his eyes. Azazel smiled warmly at him and welcomed him into her chamber. He walked in and commented on how serene everything looked. Azazel thanked him and motioned to the table, where Antonio went over to pull out her chair for her, and she took it graciously, impressed by him already.

As they sat down, they commented on how great the dinner looked, and Antonio reached across the table to open the bottle of wine, which was perfectly chilled by the time the cork popped and two flutes were poured. Azazel watched Antonio take over to make sure that she was comfortable in her own room with him. It was refreshing and made her feel very taken care of.

Once Antonio took his seat again, he waited for her to start her meal before he began to eat his, both commenting on the taste and how the chef had outdone himself once again. Azazel genuinely enjoyed herself, wondering why she hadn't done this earlier. After all, there *was* only one Antonio.

They continued their meal, and a million scenarios rushed through Azazel's head concerning their future and where it would go. As they finished, Antonio poured her another glass of wine, and Azazel sipped it while looking at him. He looked so handsome across from her, and he had such an easy-going nature; it was hard not to like him immensely. Antonio talked about himself, and she found out that he enjoyed reading mythology and studying, and especially enjoyed fishing. He was always charming, but now that she had gotten to know him better, she understood why everyone loved him as much as they did. He was easy to be with, and was one of the least judgmental people she had ever met. Azazel didn't want to admit it, but she felt herself falling for him very quickly.

As eager as she was to take things to the next level, she didn't want to rush into anything and could sense that

Antonio shared the same feeling. After they finished dinner, Antonio got up, came over to her, and held his hand out.

Azazel looked up at him in confusion as he asked, "Dance?"

She smiled at him, took his hand, and said, "There's no music."

He responded, "There isn't?"

Azazel was charmed and followed him to the open space behind their table. He spun her around delicately and pulled her close to him, putting his hand gently on her lower back as her hands slid up his muscular arms to hook around the back of his neck. She was immediately filled with his scent—sandalwood and cinnamon scents that filled her senses and made her feel helpless and protected in his arms.

As they danced, Antonio ran his hand up her back and toward the side of her neck, pulling her face close to his so their lips were barely touching.

He whispered, "Please, Goddess, may I?"

Azazel smiled and replied, "You may," and Antonio pulled her face to his.

His kiss was intense and passionate. He kissed her slowly and ran his other hand up her body until he was cupping her face in his hands. She responded to his pace. She nibbled his bottom lip as she pulled away, and when she opened her eyes, they looked at each other as if their entire world had been shaken.

Antonio went to pull her in for another kiss, but she held her hand up and stopped him by his chest. "Goodnight, Antonio." She watched his face fall in slight disappointment but noticed that his eyes were shining. He walked toward the door, and he looked back at her to grab her hand and bring it up to his mouth.

He lightly kissed the back, and as he pulled it away from

his face, Azazel stuck a finger out to stroke his cheek as it passed. She wanted him, and his body language screamed that he felt the same. Antonio paused, and Azazel smiled at him when she said, "I had a wonderful night, Antonio. Thank you."

He paused for a moment before he replied, "As did I, Goddess... although we didn't discuss any form of agreement." He looked at her with a hint of worry.

Azazel grabbed his forearm. "I thought it was clear," she said quietly to him.

Antonio swallowed hard and stuttered, "Maybe I need more clarification."

Azazel stepped closer to him and smirked when she said, "I like when you're nervous," and pulled him back in for a longer kiss that left Antonio silent for a few moments after Azazel pulled away.

Antonio opened his eyes and nodded to her. "Yes, crystal clear now."

Azazel assumed he meant that he was open to their relationship going to the next level. As he left her chamber, he reached back to squeeze her hand once more before letting himself out of her room. Once the door was shut, Azazel went around the room, blowing out each candle and putting them on the dressing table to let them cool until they were ready to be put back into the cabinet. She couldn't wipe the smile off of her face, the whole night replaying in her mind—the smell of Antonio and how he touched her and led her around as they danced. He was perfect and the most complementary addition to her image.

Walking back into her closet, she got herself undressed and didn't realize that she had put the dress and shoes back in their spots. She was so preoccupied with thinking of Antonio's lips on hers that she completed her servants' duties for them, but Azazel didn't mind. She was a different kind of happy and looked forward to the future she could build with Antonio.

Azazel selected a long white nightgown and pulled it over her head. The silk felt so lovely as it settled against her skin. Continuing to the bathroom to finish her nighttime routine, Azazel noticed that one of her hands was starting to form an age spot in the light. Her mouth turned downwards, wondering how that could be possible. She had just absorbed that whiny steward a mere twenty-four hours ago!

She tried to push her concern out of her head; she would be replenished soon and wouldn't have to worry about trivial things like aging. Continuing back to her luxurious bed, she pulled the heavy covers over herself and crawled under the sheets. She closed her eyes, and her dreams were filled with sweet kisses and dancing to no music.

8

Upon opening her eyes the following morning, Azazel's heart started to flutter when the memories of her first kiss with Antonio came rushing into her mind like it had been waiting all night for her. Azazel hurriedly got out of bed and ran to get dressed. She needed to wear the perfect outfit today!

As she zipped up her dress, she remembered that it was the day of the big feast, the large carnival-style meal that would last all night and into the morning, celebrating the combatants and their talents. They would all be showcasing different fighting styles to boost donations from their sponsors. A smile spread across her face when she realized that an exciting day was ahead of her.

Looking at herself in the mirror, she knew instantly that the navy bandage dress with the sweetheart neckline was a perfect choice. She loved the embellishments that gathered the material at her waist, making her look even more like an hourglass. Azazel touched her neck, wondering about jewelry for a second before remembering that Antonio's necklace would look *perfect* with her dress. Then again, she thought Antonio's necklace would look perfect with any attire.

Putting the necklace on and then grabbing a pair of silver strappy stiletto platforms, she finished her look and smiled at herself until the age spot on her hand caught her attention. Frowning, she realized it was darker than the night before. She sighed; thankfully, she would see Monica, who would have something to cover up the dark mark. She moved past her worry and returned to her excited state as she left her chamber to go into her makeup room.

As Azazel walked into the room, she was pleased to see that Monica was just getting to her station. Monica asked how the special dinner went, which sent Azazel into an excited storytelling tirade. She left out the final kiss, however. But the story was still enough to make Monica show her excitement for Azazel's new love interest.

Monica motioned to the chair, and Azazel sat down, brushing her hair behind her shoulders. She asked if Monica had anyone in her life, which led Monica to open up and share that she had a husband and two children, to which she paused, and Azazel pried, asking why she was hesitating. Monica then told her about her children's illnesses and worried about them eventually being selected for the Cunning. Azazel listened intently and could feel the fear radiating from her artist.

When Monica was done, her voice quivered with emotion, and Azazel locked eyes with her in the mirror, promising her that she would never hear her children's names be called. Azazel was relieved that Monica confided in her about her children. She didn't want to absorb sick combatants; they left an awful taste in her mouth, and their soul essence wouldn't do anything for rejuvenation. Monica felt like they had grown closer and had a newfound respect for her leader, and Azazel was taking a mental note of who was going to make up for Monica's family.

While Monica was working on Azazel's face, she mentioned the age spot on her hand, which Monica quickly covered up to ease Azazel's worries. When she finished, she told Azazel to open her eyes slowly. When Azazel opened her eyes fully, she was taken back by how beautiful the makeup was. Monica had done a long cat-eye with very subtle earthy tones. The eyelashes she used were long and luscious, and framed Azazel's eyes in the sultriest way. She was pleased that Monica had finished the look with a deep red lipstick and had straightened her hair to fall down the middle of her back. She looked sophisticated and powerful. It was one more look that Monica had perfected. Azazel thanked her and walked out of the room, intending to go to the master list maker to tell him of the newfound information from Monica.

As she walked down the hall, she felt her entire staff watching her. Mesmerized by her beauty that morning, she soaked it in and smiled at them all. Azazel finally came to the master list maker's quarters and knocked on the door three times. She heard crashing and rummaging around behind the door. Finally, a flustered, stout man with a handlebar mustache opened the door, and his face was red, his clothes disheveled.

"Goddess, what a surprise!" he exclaimed.

Azazel pushed the door open and walked in. "List Maker, I need you to make an adjustment."

The short man started to wring his hands together and muttered nervously, "An adjustment, your highness?" As he walked over to his cluttered desk and started to pile up loose pieces of paper, Azazel watched him.

"Yes, I need you to take a family name off the grand selection list for the next fifty years or so." She then turned her attention to her nails, inspecting them while the list maker looked around for the grand list.

He pushed everything off his desk and unrolled the scroll when he found it. Azazel looked at him and then around at his chamber. Tall bookshelves were lining the entire room, each shelf overflowing with scrolls or thick books. Azazel wondered what they all were, and before she could ask, the list maker grabbed a quill and waited for further direction.

Azazel looked at the list. "I don't know her last name, but it's my makeup artist, Monica. I wish to take her family's name off of the list."

She smiled, but that quickly turned into a frown when the list maker replied, "I am truly sorry, your eminence, but I cannot take the name off of the list if we do not know the name." He trailed off.

Azazel stood up and straightened her dress. "That sounds like it's your problem now. I expect it done." And she let herself out of the room.

Pleased that she had completed her good deed for the day, Azazel decided she would treat herself to a sweet breakfast before she went to find Antonio in the kingdom. Sitting at the breakfast table, Azazel thought of everything that had happened over the past twenty-four hours and was pleased with the direction that her life was heading. She never knew any simple pleasures in Heaven, and she liked Earth solely for the simple pleasures that it offered.

Popping a crunchy grape into her mouth, Azazel savored the taste and ate the entire plate of fruit. When she finished, she downed a mug of peppermint tea, and then left the dishes in her spot. Her chambermaids had a leisurely morning because she did most of their work for them. Azazel would not be making that mistake again for the kitchen staff.

As Azazel opened the grand front doors, Antonio was just about to knock, and they both blushed when they saw each other. Antonio ran his hand through his hair and smiled as he looked down to the ground. Azazel was giddy that Antonio was so nervous around her. She cleared her throat and motioned to his arm.

"Care to walk me down?"

When he gladly agreed, they linked together and strolled through the garden, wanting to prolong having to separate again, but they eventually came to the gates. Antonio dropped his arm, motioning for his leader to walk through the gate first, to which Azazel obliged and was a little sad that their moment had to come to an end, even though it made it all the more exciting that it was a secret.

They walked the streets; Antonio walked slightly behind her, watching as people brought up more flowers and garlands as offerings to Azazel. By the time they reached her throne, Antonio was completely covered in flowers, and other members of different families had to come to help him. When Azazel and Antonio could finally see each other again, she discreetly winked at him, and when he smiled at her, she felt nervous and excited.

Turning her attention back to the kingdom, she waited for the area around her throne to fill up with people before Antonio's father, Louis, brought forward the large bell that signaled it was time to start the grand feast. Azazel lifted the bell and rang it loudly, sending the crowd into a frenzy as they brought different types of food to the front of the crowd while others brought tables and chairs. Azazel looked around at her kingdom, and for the first time in a very long time, she felt at peace and like everything was going the way she wanted them to.

9

Aloud siren sounded as the kingdom came together for the feast, and the first bites were taken. The combatants all went out of the training arena one by one as the trainer announced their current stats and strengths, with some family background sprinkled in to make them more attractive. Azazel watched everyone and would look back to Antonio to see if he seemed to favor one more than another. But he was hard to read in this setting. Still, it made her happy that he had a soft side just for her, and she was excited to see more of it.

After the final combatant came out, they all took their places at the long table nearest to Azazel. She wished everyone well and blessed the night, telling everyone to eat their fill and be merry.

The crowd erupted into thunderous applause, and Azazel smiled. Even though she knew they had no choice in loving her, she would never grow tired of the deafening love they showed her when she wanted them to. Motioning for them to quiet down, she again encouraged them to show the warriors love and gratitude for their immense sacrifice. She wanted the kingdom to be surrounded by love and have a peaceful atmosphere.

Her playthings turned back to their dinners, and the conversation dulled down to a mumble amongst the crowd. As she turned to go back to her throne, Antonio was suddenly behind her, and she greeted him warmly and motioned toward the crowd, asking him to accompany her, to which he agreed happily.

As they made their way down the combatant's table, acknowledging everyone with small talk, Azazel felt like she wanted to go back to her palace for a short while to recharge. She told Antonio that she wouldn't be very long and requested that he stay there and watch over things for her. His ego made him answer quicker than he would have probably liked, but she trusted him and knew he would ensure things went smoothly.

Turning to leave the crowd, Azazel looked forward to having some alone time. She felt depleted suddenly and walked as fast as she could back to her home, ignoring all the staff she walked past.

When she finally made it back, she called for a glass of water to be brought to her as she walked into her chamber. She felt like she was out of breath. Azazel went over to her bed, and as she passed a mirror on a dresser, she almost screamed when she saw that her skin looked loose and wrinkled. Azazel ran to the mirror and smeared her hands over her face and through her hair, only to pull out large clumps of hair. She screamed at such a decibel that she shattered the mirror and the windows in her room.

She collapsed onto the floor and started crying when she heard a loud knock at the door, and Monica came into the room slowly. Looking at Azazel on the floor and the mirror shards surrounding her, she rushed in, carefully stepping over the sharp pieces. When she made it to Azazel, she dropped down beside her and reached out to her.

"Goddess, what happened?" This caused Azazel to sob harder. Monica could barely make out "I'm aging," which caused Monica to pause before she said, "Well, we all do."

But this caused Azazel to turn on her sharply as she seethed, "I don't!" She slowly started to get up and continued, "I am not some pathetic meat suit. I am divine, something stupid humans will never truly understand!"

Monica stood up, clearly offended. "With all due respect, Goddess, but we are not pathetic."

Azazel came close to her. "Oh, no?" And she started to force Monica to walk through the shattered shards backward. As Azazel followed her, her feet began to bleed profusely after two steps. "You really don't think your species is anything more than livestock?" Monica watched as Azazel's pupils dilated, and her eyes turned completely black.

Monica started to stammer, "Goddess, please, I'm sorry. I meant no harm!"

But Azazel was beyond reasoning. She pushed Monica onto the floor and got on top of her. Monica started to cry and scream before Azazel covered her mouth and came close to her ear. "If you scream one more time, I will make this as painful as possible for you. Nod if you understand." Monica nodded quickly, and Azazel looked her in the eyes as she said, "Good."

Azazel stood up over Monica and told her to stay put.

Monica listened, but she was whimpering as she watched Azazel go over to her nightstand and pull out a vial. Azazel returned quickly and straddled Monica again, chuckling.

"You could have gotten up and left, but you wouldn't because you couldn't."

Monica was confused, and she asked, "What do you mean, Goddess? Why are you doing this?"

Azazel opened the vial and looked down at her. "Because sooner or later, toys get old, and I get bored—"

Monica quickly interrupted. "Toys?"

Azazel sighed loudly, clearly annoyed. "Because I like you, Monica, I'll quickly tell you, but then we need to get this over with. The longer we drag this out, the worse it will be for you."

Monica nodded. "Please. Tell me."

Azazel set the vial beside them and started, "I use this kingdom as my personal farm-to-table service." And this caused Monica to gasp loudly. Azazel shushed her. "I've taken your sons off the master list, but unfortunately, sweet Monica, someone from your family needs to step forward. I don't see anyone else here but you." This caused Monica to sob, and she started begging for her life.

Azazel looked at the vial beside them, and soon decided that after everything Monica had done for her look, she was worthy. She leaned forward, kissed Monica's forehead, and placed her hands on her chest, where they started to glow white. Instantly, Monica went limp.

After some time, Azazel felt Monica's lungs collapse, and the orb finally came out of Monica's mouth, to which Azazel deeply inhaled. Azazel's hair grew back, and she watched as the skin on her arms and mouth tightened up and looked youthful once again.

Once she felt normal again, she stood up and looked down at Monica, who had a smile on her face. Azazel was annoyed that she'd now have to find another makeup artist and stepped over Monica's body.

Walking out of her chamber, she went into the kitchen, where she knew the Head of Staff would be, overseeing the cooking of the excellent meal for her kingdom. When Azazel spotted him near the head chef, she weaved her way through the kitchen until she reached him and pulled him to the side.

She only had to say, "New makeup artist" for him to understand.

He nodded and replied, "I will get right on it."

Azazel smiled and thanked him for working as hard as he was. She decided that she wanted to go back to the celebration, but she would push the Cunning up to take place in the next several days instead of weeks. Seeing herself age like that scared her, and she didn't know what was happening.

As she made her way back to the meal, no one was paying attention to her as she passed. They were all focused on the food in front of them and trying to catch a glimpse of the combatants. Azazel walked through the crowd with immense purpose and up onto her throne's platform, calling for everyone to quiet down. She announced that while there were already many surprises in store for this year's Cunning, she wanted to throw one more surprise into the works—that the Cunning would take place in the next couple of days. She felt that the combatants were ready, and she wanted to put their skills to the test.

This caused the entire kingdom to roar in surprise and excitement. Azazel watched as the combatants looked at each other, and she could feel the tension rise. She spent the rest of the night talking to the combatants, encouraging them, and preparing them for the Cunning. She made sure to make every one of them feel special before she moved on to the next. Once she had spoken to the last warrior and the sun started to rise in the sky, Antonio came over and put his hand softly on Azazel's back while he leaned in to say, "Goddess, shall we move on?"

Azazel beamed at him and nodded. He led her to the section where all the families waited for her with an early morning spread.

Florence Li brought forward a large cup of chai tea and offered it to Azazel, who took it and thanked the elderly woman with immense sincerity. The hot liquid was the perfect addition to her new look. Antonio came up and put his jacket around her shoulders, making many family members exchange looks.

He quickly backtracked. "You looked like you were starting to get cold, Goddess. I don't mean to offend." As he bowed low, Azazel thanked him and commended him on his thoughtfulness.

Azazel talked with the families about the potential bets and where the money would be sent. She wasn't surprised when many of her courtiers were placing bets on Thomas O'Donoghue, and was thrilled when she concluded that he may just win the prize. The whole community had faith in him, regardless of how superficial the belief may be.

Once everyone finished eating, they all started to slowly make their way back to their homes, and Azazel looked forward to getting into her bed. Antonio stayed back and asked her if she wanted him to walk her back to her chamber. She couldn't help but notice his hopeful look, and she hated to disappoint him, but she wasn't sure if Monica had been cleaned up yet or not and didn't want to risk him seeing anything.

Instead, Azazel told him that she would send for him later, and they could have tea in the afternoon. Antonio took her hand, kissed it softly, sending shivers down her spine, and walked away, telling her that he was looking forward to it. Azazel waited until she couldn't see him anymore and walked home quickly, wondering what she was going home to.

She was almost running by the time she got to her palace and tried to stay as calm as possible. When Azazel opened her bedroom door, she was thrilled to see that Monica's body had been taken away, and the mirror had been cleaned up, with a new one taking the broken one's place. Azazel was satisfied with the results and looked forward to meeting her new makeup artist.

Getting ready for bed, she thought of Monica—not the absorption but all of their shared times over the years. Even though she physically wasn't here anymore, Azazel knew that Monica would have wanted to sacrifice herself for her children in the end anyway if she really had a choice. At least Azazel gave her the knowledge and peace of mind that her children would be safe and taken care of; it's the best gift a mother could ever receive.

As Azazel settled into her bed, she lied back on her plush pillows, and Monica's smile floated in and out of her head as she started to relax, beckoning sleep to come. She felt satisfied and, most importantly, youthful. She closed her eyes and let out a sigh, hoping this was one of the last nights she would sleep alone.

10

Opening her eyes the following day, Azazel had a weird feeling. She didn't know what it was, but she felt this day would be different. She decided that she would have a bath before she left her room. She didn't want to be disturbed, so she went into her bathroom and turned the faucet on. Azazel sighed and rubbed the back of her neck. Tossing and turning all night caused her sleep to become restless, and she already decided that she would be taking a nap that day; Azazel wanted the day to be as stress-free as possible. She decided she would stay around the palace and have Antonio oversee the training in her place, making herself smile instantly when she thought of Antonio and felt a little better.

Going over to her closet, Azazel pulled out lavender and chamomile drops and put them into the bath. Grabbing Epsom salts and some delicious smelling oil, she made the most luxurious bath for herself. She sighed and dropped down into the comforting bathwater; she couldn't help but think that she had never had to absorb people while waiting for the Cunning. When Azazel thought back to the steward, she wondered if he had some sort of ailment that caused the absorption to not take full effect. Azazel rolled her eyes at the thought of the whiny, pathetic steward, of course. It's his fault; even in death, he was an inconvenience.

She let her head fall back and tried to push him out of her mind; he was gone, and there was no reason she should still be thinking about him. Grabbing a bar of soap and a plush loofa, she soaped her body up, taking her time and enjoying every second. Once she felt clean, she lifted the drain plug and got out of the tub. She grabbed her towel off the rack beside her and wrapped it around her body, and felt like she was wrapping herself in a cloud. The towels were exceptionally soft this morning.

Walking into her closet, she decided to pick out a pair of black silk shorts and a white tank top, letting her hair stay down to air-dry. Azazel sent word that she would be taking her meals in her chamber and that Antonio would be the official presence at the training arena.

It wasn't long before there was a quiet knock on the door, and the kitchen staff brought in a table and various trays of fruit for her. The final staff member brought in a mint green teapot and cup. She was relieved that no one was talking to her or trying to interact with her. Azazel did notice, however, that no one would look her in the face. They all kept their distance and seemed to veer out further to avoid her. She wondered if they had found out about Monica, and that was the reason. But she didn't want to alarm anyone, so she kept her distance, watching them come in and out of her room. Once the last staff member left her room, she went over to the table, ate the fruit platter, and drank the tea in peaceful silence.

Azazel went to a stack of books on top of her dresser and picked up a poetry book. She whispered, "Yes, this is perfect," took her cup of tea, and got back into bed, slowly reading each page and enjoying her time. She couldn't remember the last time she took some time for herself, but she had a feeling that she should be doing it more often.

Genuinely captivated by her book, she didn't hear the initial knock when it sounded. When it sounded a bit more urgent and heavier, Azazel let out a sigh when she called out, "Enter," to which the door slowly opened.

The Head of Staff stuck his head in and asked, "Goddess, I know you want some time alone today, but do you have a moment?"

Azazel motioned for him to come in and told him to shut the door. As he got closer to the bed, Azazel could see that he had dark circles under his eyes. He didn't sleep, either. When he stopped at her bed, Azazel held a finger up, telling him she wanted to finish the page that she was on. He waited patiently for her to finish.

When Azazel closed the book, she left her finger to mark where she left off, folded her other hand on top of the book, and looked up to her Head of Staff. "Yes, Mulligan?"

He seemed thrown off and stuttered, "I apologize, Goddess, but I wanted to let you know that your new makeup artist is here." He looked down, and Azazel watched him fidget with his clothing.

"Is there anything else?" she asked and got even more nervous when he told her, "Last night, I came to take care of the issue in your chamber. But when I got here, there were two chambermaids already here. I didn't catch the redhead's name, but the other was Sarika. They were both in hysterics upon finding Monica's body."

Azazel nodded. "So, would you rather me handle them then, Mulligan? Or would you like to do the job I paid you to do?" She opened her book back up.

"I killed them, Goddess," and Azazel looked up and asked him to repeat himself. He told her that the two chambermaids in question were notorious gossipers. The entire kingdom would have known what happened if he had let them live.

Azazel put the book off to the side and digested the information she was just told. When she looked up to her Head of Staff, he had a guilty look on his face, and she understood.

"You're confessing because you want to be punished?"

Not sure how to proceed, Mulligan looked up at Azazel and was surprised to see a look of amusement on her face. He started to tell her no when she interrupted him.

"Mulligan, you cleaned up a mess. It's your job. Good job," and she picked up the book to flip back to her place. Mulligan stood there, slightly confused. She looked at him over her book and asked, "Is there anything else, Mulligan?"

He shook his head and bowed. "Thank you, Goddess."

But after he left her room, Azazel couldn't help but think about what just happened, concluding that his services may come in handy later.

She finished the book and decided that she wanted some more fruit, and walked out of her room toward the dining room. Thankfully, when she walked by, the staff were just starting to bring platters of food out to the table, platters filled with berries and melons. Azazel took it from her and went back to her room, planning to take her time and enjoy every bite.

Focused on the tray, Azazel didn't even notice Antonio standing in her room when she first got back to her chamber. As she turned around, she gasped, and he bowed low, apologizing for startling her. Azazel reassured him, explaining she didn't expect anyone to be here. They both laughed, and Azazel walked over to her bed and set the platter down before she climbed in between the sheets. Antonio shuffled from foot to foot and looked down. Azazel pulled the platter onto her lap and tapped the space beside her.

"Come sit," she beckoned him.

Antonio obliged and sat beside Azazel as she started to eat a piece of melon. After swallowing the initial piece and sighing in pleasure, she held the platter out to Antonio, offering him some. He graciously took a strawberry, and the two ate while talking about how things were going around the kingdom in preparation for the Cunning.

Azazel finished a piece of watermelon and turned to Antonio. "How did the training go today?" she asked eagerly.

Antonio smiled and grabbed another piece of fruit. "You are going to be incredibly pleased," he replied before popping the fruit into his mouth.

Azazel nodded. "Yes, I knew that. But who do you think is going to win, Antonio?"

He paused before finally saying, "Well, after today, it could be any one of them. They all have a killer instinct, and it is truly a sight to behold."

Azazel was thrilled to hear this, smiling as she looked at Antonio. "Thank you for taking my place today."

Antonio nodded and looked around. "Have you just been resting today, Goddess?"

Azazel nodded and corrected him. He said her name. Azazel loved hearing him say it, and the feeling it gave her when he did. They finished the platter, and Antonio asked if she needed him for anything else. Azazel looked at him with so much admiration and declined, telling him that she just needed the day to rest, and she would be back to her duties the next morning. She asked him if he had any plans for the day, to which he told her that he was overseeing the inventory change for his home as they prepared for the changing season. Azazel was taken with how simple the task sounded and commended Antonio for being involved with his family's caretaking.

Leaving his beautiful goddess smiling, Antonio also mentioned that he was looking forward to seeing her around the kingdom and counted down the moments until they could share another dance. Antonio's charm worked the way it was supposed to, and she told him that she would send word for him when she could fit him into her schedule. He bowed and winked at her as he left her smiling in her bed.

Azazel felt content with how comfortable they were becoming around each other already. Even though he seemed to make her nervous, being with him felt so easy. She spent the rest of her day drifting in and out of sleep. Her dreams were plagued with faces from past Cunnings that she had absorbed.

When she woke up the final time, she was in a cold sweat and couldn't figure out why she would dream of them, looking around and noticing that it had become dark outside. Azazel was slightly concerned that she had slept for so long, but her body clearly needed it. And she was starting to get annoyed of her dreams. She had never thought of the humans *after* the absorption.

Getting out of bed, Azazel walked into the kitchen to grab a glass of water. As she walked down the dark hallway, she couldn't help but notice how eerie everything felt when the staff weren't constantly moving around.

As she walked into the kitchen, she was lost on the location of the glasses and started opening up cabinets to find them until she did. Once she filled her cup and took a sip, she looked around and wondered why there wasn't a skeleton crew for nighttime. She would speak to Mulligan the next day and put a change in place right away. She felt she deserved to be waited on at all hours of the day *and* night. Once she finished her drink, she put the glass on the counter and returned to her bedroom. As she walked across her room where Monica's body once was, she concluded that she would bring Mulligan in as a clean-up crew for the Cunning. He was incredibly good at his job.

11

The following day, Azazel opened her eyes and sprang from her bed. She chose to wear a dark pencil skirt with a ruffled white blouse. She spent very little time inspecting herself in the mirror and headed directly to the makeup room. And she was surprised to see a man standing inside, waiting for her. He was as tall as she was and had a blue tinge to his hair, his bottom lash line was lined in back, and he had glitter on his cheekbones, wearing black pants and a bright yellow shirt with several necklaces. Azazel checked him out and was instantly obsessed with him

He bowed low and held his hand out to the chair. "Goddess." When she sat down, he looked at her in the mirror and asked, "Shall I show you what I can do?"

He grabbed a brush to start brushing her hair. Azazel smiled and nodded. She knew it was going to be incredible. She shut her eyes and let herself be hypnotized by his gentle motions, knowing she would look stunning when he was done. Azazel thought of the many mornings spent here with Monica and was sad for a moment. She really did consider her to be a friend, but desperate times called for desperate measures, and this way, Monica would always be a part of her. Azazel comforted herself with the final thought and focused on what she was going to do today.

While Monica was beautiful, and Azazel felt rejuvenated, she wasn't sure how long Monica's essence would keep her feeling that way, and she felt a slight pang of desperation. She wasn't sure how long she sat there for, and while Azazel was so lost in her thoughts, this new artist didn't bother her with questions or try to bond with her. Azazel liked it.

Finally, he made the final touches and told her she was ready. When Azazel opened her eyes, her breath was taken away. He had put red glitter over her lipstick and used warm tones around her eyes with heavy smoked-out black eyeliner and dramatic cat-eye lashes. Her hair was twisted into a messy fishtail braid that wrapped around her shoulder and rested nicely over her chest.

She leaned forward and wouldn't give him the satisfaction of pleasing her early in their professional relationship.

She simply said, "It's not bad."

"Dante," he told her. "The name's Dante."

Azazel replied, "I didn't ask."

He bowed as he said, "You look absolutely fabulous, Goddess."

Azazel got up and walked past him, and as she was about

to step out of the door, she looked back to him and said, "We are going to get along wonderfully, Dante."

She strutted down the hall for a few minutes before realizing that she was missing the sound of heels tapping against the floor. Azazel looked down and realized that she hadn't grabbed shoes for the day. Quickly turning around, she walked to her chamber and selected a pair of light pink studded stilettos.

This time, she took her time looking at herself in the mirror. She was obsessed with herself, and she knew that everyone who came into contact with her that day would be taken by her beauty. As she walked past the makeup room, she glanced in to see Dante spraying sanitizer on a brush, and she liked him even more.

Walking past the dining room, she was excited and decided she would take a late lunch instead. Maybe she would invite Antonio and pick up where they left off. Azazel smiled, knowing he would be intrigued by her appearance.

As she walked down the street, she couldn't help but notice how quiet it was. No citizens were coming out to greet her, and the stores seemed incredibly quiet. Azazel picked the pace up and was relieved when she saw a large crowd outside the training arena. The crowd parted for her as she made her way through it, all bowing to her. She made it all the way to the makeshift stage set-up, and as she stepped onto the first step, the trainer came out of the building and started to walk up a staircase on the other side of the stage. He came over and bowed low.

When he stood up, he said, "You look absolutely radiant today, Goddess," and Azazel thanked him and mentioned that she hoped he had good news for her.

The trainer smiled and said, "We will have to see, Goddess," and walked toward the microphone in the middle of the stage.

Azazel motioned with her arms for the crowd to quiet down, and once they were silent, she looked at the trainer, who began speaking and welcoming the people for coming once again. The combatants all went out of the arena and lined up in four rows. The crowd was pushed back as they all took their spots. Once they were lined up, they stood straight and faced forward.

The trainer announced to the crowd that the Cunning would be moved up to take place in three days. During the next few days, the combatants would spend time with their families and sponsors, and come back daily for training. With Azazel's blessing, she nodded enthusiastically, which caused the crowd to erupt in thunderous applause.

Azazel hadn't seen Antonio yet, but she wanted to spend some time with him. She decided that she would take the time and relax a little more. She planned to do a cleansing ritual before absorbing any of the combatants. Her stomach started to flutter in excitement when she thought of the feast that she would be having soon.

The trainer finally stopped speaking and looked over at Azazel, asking if she needed to add anything. When she said no, he pulled out his whistle and blew it three times, and the combatants all broke their lines and went off to their families, who welcomed them back loudly with last names being shouted in pride. The adrenaline made the air thick, and Azazel thrived on the scent in the atmosphere. This year's Cunning was going to be one for the history books.

Once the crowd started to thin out, Azazel stepped down the stairs and walked away from the arena until she came to the perfumery. Thankfully, they were already open and working away in the store as she opened the door and let herself in.

The smell was warm and comforting, and she knew she wanted whatever scent *that* was. The store owner welcomed her and asked her what she was looking for. Azazel told her that she was looking for hair and body oils. The store owner quickly walked to the back and brought two elaborate bottles back with her, saying that they contained the best patchouli and cinnamon, which is currently in the air. Azazel was pleased and told her to send the bill up to the palace, to which the store owner replied that it was her pleasure to give them to Azazel.

Azazel was touched and pledged that she would be a regular customer and gave the store owner Mulligan's direct contact number. The store owner was surprised and thanked her profusely. Azazel left the store, and the owner danced excitedly. She was in a great mood and knew she would smell otherworldly.

She walked slowly toward her palace and noticed a family walking with a combatant. The parents had their arms around the girl, and she seemed at ease. Azazel was pleased to see the combatants so happy. Happy souls were usually better for her in the long run.

Walking through the garden, the smell of roses was overpowering, and Azazel decided to stop and admire how full they were blooming this year. She definitely needed to have the staff members decorate the palace with these flowers.

She made her way to the kitchen when she got back to the palace, and found the head chef behind a pot of steaming sauce. Azazel requested something rich and chocolatey, to which the chef replied that he would be able to come up with something delicious for her. She left the kitchen, looking forward to what he would come up with.

She walked by the makeup room and noticed that Dante wasn't in there, and the light was off. She frowned in concern. Monica never left the room during the day. Not wanting to dwell too much on the whereabouts of her staff,

Azazel continued to her room, where she found two new chambermaids dusting and straightening her room up.

Azazel smiled and asked that one of them go and pick the roses. They both started exclaiming how beautiful the flowers were, and how they would truly elevate the decor in the palace. They both left the room, and Azazel went to set the oils in her bathroom. She put the bottles on the counter and was almost blinded by the light caught in the thick glass. She was mesmerized by the beauty and looked forward to filling her bathroom with more bottles.

12

When Azazel returned to her room, one of the chambermaids came rushing in with a large bouquet and was out of breath. Azazel smiled at her and was touched that she had worked so quickly to make her goddess happy. She walked over to her cabinet to get a vase and took the flowers from her maid, thanking her for her hard work. The chambermaid curtsied and ran out of the room. Azazel filled the vase with water and placed it beside her bed. The roses looked like they bloomed even more since she initially saw them.

She grabbed another book from her shelf; Azazel went and lied on her bed and started to read, becoming lost in the story and losing track of time. There was a light knock on the door, and when she told them to come in, she was pleased to see the head chef bringing in a plate. Sitting up, she was eager to see what he had in store for her. When he put the plate down, she saw it was a pastry blossom, but it looked like the pastry was chocolate, and then the chef went on to tell her that there was a heated chocolate ganache and raspberry purée in the center. Azazel looked forward to eating the treat before her and thanked the chef for another edible work of art.

When he left, she picked up the plate and dug her fork in the middle of the pastry to pull it apart, forcing the gooey and decadent insides to come spilling out all over the plate. Azazel's eyes widened with excitement, and when she took the first bite, she was transported to a world of delicious pleasure. Her intention of slowly enjoying the desert went out the window, and she finished it within moments.

After she finished, she put the plate off to the side and grabbed the book she had started before. She didn't read it for very long. There was an urgent knock on the door, and she told them to come in. Mulligan came rushing into her chamber, exclaiming that one of the combatants was trying to leave the kingdom. Azazel thought he was joking at first, but when she looked up and saw his panicked face, she realized that she was needed.

Quickly getting out of bed, she put on a pair of hard-bottomed slippers and ran outside. Thankfully, Azazel didn't need to run far, and she ran into a crowd of people led by the trainer, who had the rogue combatant by the scruff of her shirt. It was the girl she had seen earlier that day. Scanning the crowd for her parents, Azazel announced that she would take the girl and the parents back to the palace to get to the bottom of this.

As the parents came forward, they wrapped their arms

around the girl, and Azazel watched as they all collapsed to the ground. Trying to keep her emotions under control, Azazel tried to show compassion instead of the inner rage she was trying to keep a lid on. She ushered them back to her home and led them into the back garden, where there was a gazebo covered with ivy and a table with four chairs underneath it.

They all took a seat, and Azazel simply asked, "Are you not proud of your daughter?"

The parents, who were quick to offer their praise and thanks, mentioned that she was only fourteen and had so much life to live. Azazel looked at the combatant, who she learned was named Deanna Morgan, and asked if she didn't feel the honor that the rest of her combatant peers felt. Deanna claimed she was incredibly honored but scared, saying she had been losing every sparring match.

Deanna was nervous to see how that would fare against her competitors in the Cunning event. Azazel listened and nodded, trying to come up with a solution. She listened to the family's list of reasons as to why Deanna should be spared, and how she could contribute to the kingdom when she's older to make up for it. Azazel sighed, stood up, and began speaking, requesting them to be silent until she finished. They all leaned forward, eager to hear her.

"Every year, I have at least one family trying to find a loophole in the system and fail. Frankly, I'm tired of people not realizing what one day of sacrifice does for them throughout the rest of the year." Azazel watched the color in the parents' faces drain as she continued. "Now, each family contributes the way they are supposed to, and have done so since I came into power. It is what makes our kingdom work the way it does."

Deanna started quietly sobbing, realizing there was no way out of this, and her parents began to object. This caused Azazel to get frustrated, and she quickly placed the palms of her hands on the parents. They started to glow. Deanna watched in horror as Azazel fed a sentence into her parents' heads, and they repeated it, agreeing that the Cunning was a necessity, and they were beyond honored to be a part of it.

Azazel then turned her attention to Deanna, who started to scream before Azazel's glowing hands rested on her head, and Deanna repeated, "It is my honor and privilege to be able to compete in the Cunning. Whether I win or lose, I am an important component, and I know that my goddess appreciates my sacrifice."

Azazel smiled and pulled back from the family, pleased that they could all come to an agreement together. The family then stood up and ushered Deanna out of the garden, all three of them speaking excitedly about fighting strategies and ways that Deanna could use her small size to her advantage.

Azazel watched them leave the grounds and sighed. She didn't understand why every human needed so much reassurance. It was such an ugly trait. She made her way inside to see that Mulligan had been watching from one of the hallway windows. Azazel nodded and asked him to bring Deanna to her that evening, and to tell the trainer that there would only be ninety-nine combatants this year.

When Mulligan mentioned that someone would be left without a partner, Azazel said, "That's something for the trainer and the new steward to figure out. We do have a new steward, don't we?"

Mulligan quickly explained that he'd been rushed to find so many new staff members that he completely forgot about the steward. Azazel nodded and told him that she expected a new steward by the following day. She explained that she wanted a competent one, one who would be able to deliver a festival beyond her wildest dreams, and one to keep her on her toes.

Mulligan nodded and bowed to leave. Azazel headed toward her bedroom to have a few moments alone to collect herself again. Using her divinity to get her puppets back in line always took so much energy out of her, and she needed to rest before she could face anyone else again. Avoiding eye contact with any servant she walked by, Azazel felt like she was starting to unravel. She felt angry and frustrated that she had to absorb a combatant sooner than she had initially planned, but she felt like the family was a stack of wild cards. Azazel felt like she had no other choice.

As she opened her bedroom door, she felt like her head would split open from pain. She had never experienced pain like it before and fell to the floor. She quickly shut all of the blinds and grabbed a salve to rub on her temples, hoping it would work. She soon felt her temples become heated, and slowly, the pain started to subside. Relieved, Azazel climbed into bed, not sure what was happening to her, but she felt like if she slept, maybe it would become a bit clearer when she woke up.

She tried to think of other things to help take her mind off the pain, but even Antonio's face couldn't help her. She sighed and wondered how long she would have before Deanna was brought to her. When Azazel thought of her, she was hopeful that because of her age, Deanna would give her the essence that she needed to get to the Cunning without having to absorb anyone else.

Sleep was avoiding her, and Azazel became increasingly frustrated that she hadn't fallen asleep yet. She tossed and turned, trying to reposition herself, and kept flipping the pillows to find the cooler side.

She slowed her breathing and closed his eyes, willing herself to relax and sleep. Her mind was busy with scenarios, both real and imagined, when suddenly, she had a flashback of a moment from her time in Heaven, watching her beloved God construct the Earth, and every time she tried to interject, He would shut her down. He'd tell her that her opinions and ideas were insignificant.

Azazel felt her heart break again. She didn't realize at the time how hard it was to rule over a domain and keep everyone happy, and she was starting to realize that the humans weren't satisfied with *anything* she did. Every time her sisters and her would go to Earth, they would always come across suffering communities, but still, they prayed to God to improve their lives.

But He ignored them, every time, every prayer. Azazel thought that if she could keep the humans constantly happy, her kingdom would be blissful. But that clearly didn't seem like the case anymore.

She always hated when the divine effects started to wear off, and she would have to reprogram her humans again—the fear in their eyes as they tried to figure out what had happened and why they couldn't remember the past few years. She wondered if she would ever reach a point where she would no longer have to influence them; they would just be born willing and ready. And there would no longer be any need for the Cunning. She could simply pluck them whenever she needed rejuvenation.

Azazel let the thought remain in her head, and the more she thought about it, the more she liked it. Finally, she yawned and fell asleep. For the first time in several nights, she wasn't plagued by dreams, just sweet restful sleep.

13

Azazel was woken up by Mulligan, who gently shook her arm. She gasped but realized who it was almost immediately. He said he was about to go fetch Deanna and wanted to ensure that she was ready for her meal. Azazel couldn't help but smile at him. He was truly going above and beyond for her supernatural needs, now that he knew. She told him that she wanted him to bring Deanna's parents as well, to which Mulligan nodded and told her that he would be back shortly.

Azazel sat up and stretched. She still felt tired but realized that once the absorption was done, she would be able to go back to sleep. This was a comforting thought, and Azazel got out of bed, walked over to the door, and called out for tea to be brought to her room as quickly as possible.

A quick rap sounded at the door a few minutes later, and a chambermaid brought in a serving tray with a teapot and a single teacup. Azazel was pleased when she smelled blueberry, and knew it was the chef's special blueberry tea. The maid set the tray down and quickly backed out of the room, not making eye contact with Azazel and barely speaking. Azazel thought that perhaps Mulligan had given them a dummy story about why she didn't want to be bothered, and her appreciation for Mulligan's usefulness escalated even further.

She finished her tea and felt extremely relaxed before pouring another cup. When Deanna and her parents arrive, Azazel wanted to be in the right state of mind. Deanna had trained so hard and fought so valiantly that she would make this as painless as possible. Azazel got up and went over to her bedside table to grab the single vial rolling around as she pulled the drawer open, then went over to the door to call for another tea set to be brought in. And she didn't close the door until she heard the running of feet.

Going back to her own cup, Azazel set the vial down on the table and picked up her cup, sipping the deliciously hot liquid, bringing her more comfort than the last. Just as she saw the bottom of her cup, she heard a knock on the door, and not only was it a chambermaid with the extra tea set, much to Azazel's delight, but it was Mulligan, who looked back and told Deanna and her parents to wait there. The chambermaid came in quickly, set the tea down, bowed, and promptly exited the room. Azazel grabbed the vial and opened the top of the teapot.

When she looked up, Mulligan was watching her, and he asked, "What's that?"

Azazel simply replied, "It takes the edge off," which was sufficient enough of an answer for him.

Replacing the lid and hiding the vial in the cushions of her chair, Azazel said she was ready for them. Mulligan bowed low. "Enjoy, Goddess," and he slid out the door. The family quickly came in, and Azazel smiled at them warmly. As she stood up, they bowed, and she told them to join her as she poured three cups of tea and handed each of them one as they came closer and positioned themselves on the couch. Deanna was the first to bring the cup up to her mouth and take a sip, her eyes widening at the sweet taste. Her parents quickly followed her lead. All of them exclaimed their delight in the tea and thanked her again.

"I spoke to you earlier about how I was so tired of families trying to find loopholes to get out of the Cunning. While there is no loophole, I have a way that you all can stay together. Now, in about ten seconds, your legs are going to go numb, followed by your hands, and then the rest of your body. You're going to close your eyes and become one with me," she explained to them.

Deanna's mother started to stammer a question. She looked down at her legs, scared. The father pulled both her and Deanna in close to him, and they hugged each other for as long as they could hold on before they finally slumped.

Azazel stood up and walked over to position them, so their heads were on the back of the couch. She interlocked their hands and kissed their foreheads as they shut their eyes. She crouched down and waited, seeing who would come out first, and to her surprise, Deanna's father's soul orb peeked out first. Azazel inhaled his essence, and not much later, Deanna's was next, followed closely by her mother's.

It was like he was completely in sync with Azazel because as soon as she finished, Mulligan came in through the door and began the cleaning process, and Azazel went to take a bath. Before she went into the bathroom, she asked if there was anyone else still up, and he told her that he dismissed the staff after the last tray of tea was brought in. Azazel approved and said to him that she was impressed by him. Mulligan bowed and thanked her sincerely.

She turned to the bathroom and was excited to try the new oil from that afternoon. When she opened the bottle, the bathroom was immediately filled with the smell of patchouli, and Azazel was intoxicated by the scent. Going over to the bath, she turned the hot water all the way up, pouring some of the liquid into the tub and smiling as the smell came up and seduced her senses.

Azazel turned back to put the bottle on the counter and looked at herself, and was surprised by what she saw. Peering closer, she looked like she was back in Heaven. Her skin looked like it was radiating the same glow as the sun. Her lips looked plump, and her hair was so bright that it was almost blinding. She was incredibly pleased with her results and turned back to her bath. She got undressed and slipped into the tub while the water ran, reminiscing about how quick the results of that vial were.

It was a new method, and she liked how painless it was; plus, it didn't take any of her divinity to make it work. She was definitely going to keep using it from now on. She leaned forward when the tub was sufficiently filled and turned the water off. Sinking back into the tub, Azazel loved everything that this night had to offer.

But then she suddenly frowned. She didn't feel the same connection to the family that she had with others, where it felt like they indeed became one with her. She wondered if the divinity she put into their bodies connected them the way it was supposed to, and why she didn't feel guilty about absorbing them. When she thought of Deanna, she felt a pang of sadness as the scene of her parents reaching for her in their last moments came into her head.

Azazel hated the sadness and forced it out of her head, focusing on the heavenly-smelling bath that she was in and looking forward to the Cunning.

When the water started to cool down, and she craved some more tea, Azazel got out of the bath and dried herself off. She walked into her closet, selected a light blue cotton nightgown, put it on, and wrapped herself in a plush, comfortable robe. She intended to take it as easy as possible for the night and walked out to see Mulligan standing by the door. With a confused expression on her face, Azazel asked him what he wanted.

He replied, "We have a problem."

In a condescending tone, she said, "We don't have problems here," and she walked over to the tea set without any of the poison and poured herself a cup.

But she noticed that he hadn't left yet and was uncomfortably shuffling from foot to foot.

"Fine, what is it?" she demanded.

He cautiously replied, "The extended family was made aware that they were coming here tonight."

Azazel nodded and asked him, "What's the problem?"

Mulligan explained that this would raise concern when they don't come back home.

Azazel sighed in frustration and sipped her tea, waiting for him to finish. Once he stopped talking and looked to her for an answer, Azazel set her cup down and said, "I will handle it. Thank you, Mulligan," dismissing him. She was irritated by his presence and wanted him out of her sight.

He bowed low and asked if she needed anything.

Azazel snapped, "No, because apparently, no one can complete a simple task, so I'll take care of everything myself.

Good night, Mulligan!" The tone in Azazel's voice was ice cold, and it looked like Mulligan went pale when he figured out that she was displeased with him. He left her alone with her thoughts.

14

Azazel mulled over the information that Mulligan had just told her, and she came to a solution quickly. She would give the extended family a slight touch of divinity to forget that they were even related to Deanna and her family. Smiling at her quick thinking, Azazel decided that she would go to the house after finishing her tea.

She shouted out Mulligan's name, and unsurprisingly, he came right into her room like he had been waiting for her. He asked her what she needed from him, and Azazel said she changed her mind and wanted him to find the location of all of the extended family members, tell them all to meet at one location, and she would come talk to them.

When he quickly left the room, Azazel finished her tea calmly. If she got worked up, it could be transferred to the family when she touched them, and it would end disastrously for everyone. Once she was finished, she went over to her wardrobe and picked out a bright white dress with thick spaghetti straps and a slit on the side, deciding to pair it with a pair of golden stilettos. Azazel couldn't deny how divine she looked when she looked at herself in the mirror. She was incredibly pleased with the last absorption results, turning around to inspect every angle.

When she walked out of the closet, she was happy that Mulligan wasn't standing in her room anymore. Hopefully, he did his job correctly this time and would make it as easy as possible for her moving forward.

Azazel left her chamber and started walking toward the front door, ignoring every servant who passed her and bowed. As she walked out, Mulligan came running up to her to tell her the location she was going to. Azazel cupped his cheek, telling him she was proud that he could complete a simple task on his own for once, and left him standing there with his mouth open and his face reflecting the disappointment that he felt. She kept ignoring any citizen who passed her and stayed focused on her location, knowing that the sooner she handled this, the safer she and the kingdom would be.

She eventually came to a large house and let herself through the gate. Walking up the pathway, she noticed someone looking through the curtains in the main window on the front of the house. Azazel smiled. People trying to sneak peeks of her wasn't a new concept, and instead, she kept the smile in place as she lightly knocked on the door and waited for it to be answered.

Finally, the door was opened by an older woman in her fifties with the same color hair as Deanna, but large sections were starting to gray. Azazel tried to hide her disgust when she noticed that one of the woman's eyes was milky white from blindness. The woman nodded her head in respect and apologized for not being able to bow down, crediting her age as the reason.

Azazel reassured her and told her that she wanted to talk to the family about the Cunning, and how their contribution would bring the festivities to another level. The woman grinned and opened the door wider, welcoming Azazel in enthusiastically. Azazel stepped into the dusty house and noticed a faint odor. Looking around, it seemed as if no one had cleaned up in ages. She asked if anyone else was coming, and the woman said they were all in the back room. The woman turned back and introduced herself as Martha.

Martha led Azazel to a set of thick and extravagant double doors, and she pulled one side but struggled until Azazel stepped forward and pulled the doors apart, barely using any strength. When the doors were finally opened, Azazel was face-to-face with about twenty family members, all talking amongst themselves. When Azazel entered the room, they all stopped and bowed low, except for the elderly ones.

They waited for her to begin, and when she did, Azazel noticed they all shared a stone look as if there was nothing behind their eyes. She started by telling them that Deanna was an important combatant in the Cunning and would only bring honor to their family. The longer Azazel looked around the room, the more she noticed that there weren't any adolescent generations. They were all middle-aged or part of the older generation. And she finally realized why they were so concerned about Deanna.

Azazel walked around the room and placed her hand on each of their arms, telling them that Deanna had received the highest honor imaginable, as did her parents. They were happy but wouldn't be returning to the family home. She had every family member repeat the sentence back to her, and when she finally got to Martha, the old woman asked why they wouldn't come home. Azazel told her they were in a better place, a place where everyone in the kingdom would go to, and touched her arm, smiling at the old woman as her hand began to glow.

Once Azazel confirmed that the family was at peace, and they automatically repeated the sentences she told them to, she left the house and walked back to her palace. Azazel felt depleted, and resolved that she would sleep as soon as she got home.

When she got back, she rushed to the mirror to see if her manipulation had affected her appearance at all, and was relieved when she saw that she looked as youthful as before. Changing back into the blue cotton nightgown, Azazel went to her bed and pulled the sheets back so she could climb in.

She settled into her plush pillows, thought of the night's events, and sighed. She never had to do this sort of thing before and felt worry start to creep in as she thought of her world crumbling. Trying to push the worries off to the side, Azazel closed her eyes, begging sleep to come to relieve her of her panic.

When Azazel finally fell asleep, her dreams were plagued by Deanna and her parents' lifeless eyes staring up at her. Azazel felt like she hadn't slept in years when she woke up the following morning. She got out of bed slowly and wanted to take a bath to boost her spirits.

Yawning, she moved slowly to the bathroom, turned the hot water on, and retrieved citrus-scented essential oils. She let herself fall into the water gently, and the scents of orange, lemon, and grapefruit started to saturate the steam that wafted up into her nose. Azazel smiled at the simple pleasure she felt sitting in the water.

Once she was energized and ready for the day, Azazel lifted herself out of the water and dried off. She walked into the closet with a bounce in her step, and her mood was a bit lighter than it was when she'd woken up. Walking down the hall, trying to find the perfect outfit, she settled on a soft yellow backless sundress just above her knees and a pair of white strappy wedges. Once again, she chose to wear Antonio's necklace and felt young, carefree, and feminine as she looked in the mirror one final time before leaving her closet. When she walked into her makeup room, she beamed at each servant who passed by and saw Dante waiting patiently.

Dante bowed low and welcomed her to sit on the chair. Azazel bounced over and sat down, and Dante commented on how beautiful she looked that morning, and how her eyes had a certain twinkle. She closed her eyes and gave herself over to relaxation as Dante worked his magic.

Azazel didn't have a single thought in her head for the first time in days. Instead of getting lost in her mind, Azazel listened to Dante hum and whisper to himself, working out how he wanted her makeup to turn out. When Azazel opened her eyes again, she was pleased to see a very intense smokey eye and lashes with a piece of chunky glitter in the shape of a star on random lashes. Her lips were pink and slightly overlined to make them look plumper, her cheeks were rosy yet glowing, and her hair had been loosely curled and brushed out to make it look like waves.

Dante went on to tell her that he customized the lashes himself and talked a bit more about her look. Azazel gained immense respect for him and decided to keep him around much longer than she'd kept Monica around. As she turned around to leave the room, she winked, blew a kiss at him, and left him grinning from ear to ear as she searched for Antonio.

However, she didn't have to look for very long and found

him walking toward the palace, waving at her. Azazel waved back and felt bubbly. She liked how she felt around him, and as he came closer, her heart started to beat faster. Antonio met her in the garden and bent over her hand, kissing it gently as he said, "Azazel."

She bit her bottom lip and whispered, "Antonio."

15

Azazel noticed that his eyes glittered like the stars in the darkest night sky when he stood up. She was completely taken by him!

Antonio smiled wide, "Goddess."

She quickly pulled his face closer to hers and kissed him passionately. He wrapped his arms around her waist, kissing her deeply. The two were lost in their embrace.

Azazel was the first to pull back and breathlessly asked, "How long do you have?"

Antonio smiled and started to lean in again as he whispered, "As long as you'll have me."

He pulled her face to his, and Azazel jumped up, wrapping her legs around his waist as he moved his hands under her, supporting her effortlessly. He carried her to her bed and moved on top of her as the two lost themselves to each other in lust.

She could feel his heart pumping blood, and how strong his life essence was; Azazel suddenly felt the hunger start to bubble from the deepest parts of her stomach. As Antonio kissed her clavicle, Azazel pushed him off with her foot.

"No!" she screamed breathlessly, and they looked at each other.

Antonio was on the floor, staring up at her. As he stood up, he adjusted himself, and Azazel could see that he was trying to figure out what just happened.

She reached for him, but he took a step back as he said, "I need to leave, Goddess. I do apologize."

He bowed and went to walk away before she grabbed his hand.

"No, Antonio, it's not you." She tried to find the right words so she wouldn't scare him, but he had already walked halfway across the room, wanting to leave. Azazel rushed off the bed to grab him, and he turned to her.

"I don't need to come back; this may have been a mistake." He excused himself and left her standing in her room.

Azazel watched him leave and realized that he was probably embarrassed. She grew angry and rushed to the door, screaming for Mulligan. Pacing from one side to the other, Mulligan seemed to take an eternity to reach her. Finally, she heard a knock on the door, and she beckoned for him to come in. Mulligan sheepishly entered the room and scanned the area as if he expected to see a body on the floor.

"Yes, Goddess? What can I help you with?"

Azazel stopped pacing to look at him. "Bring me the most insignificant servant we have, NOW!" She watched the color drain from his face as she walked closer to him. When he didn't instantly leave, she shouted again. "I said, fetch the most low-life servant we have in this palace, or would you like to take their place?" she hissed.

Mulligan was frightened. He wasn't staring at his ethereal goddess; he was staring at a black-eyed being with taunt pale skin and wild hair. He could see her veins prominently, and her muscles looked like they were decaying. Mulligan quickly left the room, wanting to put as much distance between himself and Azazel as possible.

While she waited, Azazel fumed. She was furious that Antonio left; she tried to keep him safe, not completely push him away! He wouldn't have been so scared if he had just waited for her to explain. He got scared because he thought it was about *him*. This caused Azazel to roll her eyes; the human ego truly was fragile.

Her thoughts were interrupted by a frantic knock on the door. She barked for them to come in, and Mulligan walked through the door with a petite brown-haired kitchen maid. Azazel quickly grabbed the maid from Mulligan and shoved him back out the door.

"Get out; we need to have a little girl talk."

He gladly left the room as quickly as he tried to enter it. Azazel gripped the small girl's forearm and felt her struggle against her as she said, "You know, there was a time when I didn't need to feast," and threw the girl across the room and onto the edge of the bed. The young girl screamed in pain, which made Azazel smile. "I forgot how much fun it was to make your kind suffer beforehand. It makes you taste so much sweeter."

The meek kitchen maid curled herself into a ball. At the same time, Azazel slowly walked toward her. When she was close enough, the maid looked up at her, begging for Azazel to spare her. Azazel pulled the girl up by her hair until her toes were barely touching the floor, and they were eye-to-eye. The servant struggled trying to touch the floor again.

Azazel came in close and whispered, "Why on earth would I spare you when I need to eat?" She threw her across the room again with such force that the girl was knocked unconscious.

Disappointed that she didn't stay awake, Azazel pouted and walked over to the lump on the floor and flipped the servant onto her back effortlessly with her foot. Stepping over her and crouching down to straddle her body, Azazel started slapping the girl's face.

"Wake up, you coward! The wolf isn't done playing yet!"

When the girl woke up, she instantly started panicking again and began to cry, begging Azazel with her life. Azazel sighed and was growing agitated. She stood up and placed one foot on each of the girl's arms to pin her down, applying enough of her weight until she heard the crunch of breaking bones and the screaming of her victim. She plopped down on the sobbing girl once again.

"Okay, now that I have your attention, no begging! It's not very feminine of you, and you're disgracing your ancestors." The girl's face was soaking wet from her tears, and Azazel felt an immense sense of pleasure seeing how scared she was. She bent down so that she was in the girl's ear and whispered, "Do you think the Creator could help you, even now? If you prayed hard enough?"

The girl nodded quickly and whispered the Lord's prayer.

Azazel quickly grabbed her throat and seethed, "When are you stupid humans going to realize that He doesn't care about anyone but Himself? He knows what you are going through and what is going to happen to you." Her face started to morph into a dark monstrous version of herself. The maid began to shake in fear as Azazel said, "God does not care about you!"

The maid was quiet, and Azazel could see that she was starting to understand. The maid looked up into Azazel's eyes. "Then why do we pray?"

Azazel laughed and shrugged. "To feed His ego. That's the only thing humans are good for, feeding God."

Before the maid could say anything else, Azazel quickly slashed the maid's throat with her nails. Blood started to pour out as the girl began to gurgle and gasp. Azazel had a strong urge, and she leaned down and licked the girl's neck to taste the blood while she waited.

The warm liquid slid down her throat and ignited something new in Azazel as she sat up. It wasn't just rejuvenation; it felt like a hole deep inside her was slowly being filled. After an entire millennium, Azazel felt like she had found what she was missing. She leaned down and started to drink from the gash in the servant's throat until she noticed a glow out of the corner of her eye, the orb beginning to float out of her victim's mouth. Azazel sat up and inhaled the orb into her; the rejuvenation process felt more powerful.

Azazel knew this time was different. After she felt healthy again, she drank from the maid's neck. She felt the blood reach her fingertips and toes, making her body tingle. She got up, leaving the husk of the maid on the floor. Azazel went over to the door, screaming for Mulligan to clean up the mess.

When she passed the large mirror, she caught a glimpse of herself. Her skin was plump and glowing with youthfulness. And even though the bottom half of her face and chest were covered in blood, she had never felt more beautiful.

She turned and looked at herself, running her hands over her body, up through the blood, and dragging it all over. Hearing a soft knock at the door, Azazel loudly said, "Come in!" and Mulligan slowly entered the room.

His eyes went wide when he saw the state of Azazel and

the victim. Azazel started to lick the blood off her fingers and then asked him, "Mulligan, did she have any family?"

Mulligan began to stutter as he replied, "Parents and a sister, Goddess."

Azazel smiled and looked at him. "Good, bring them to me tomorrow. Now, clean this up! I need to bathe." Azazel turned and left him in shock as he took in the entire scene.

Going to her bathroom and starting the hot water, Azazel decided that she didn't want to dilute the smell of her kill with anything else, and instead, got undressed and slipped into the hot water and let it wash over her. Rinsing the blood off of her, filling her nostrils with the metallic smell, Azazel was soothed and leaned back, savoring every second of it.

She could hear the bedroom door open and close multiple times and shuffling around. Azazel was thankful for her clean-up crew, but she frowned at having to deep clean the floor every time she fed. But it was all worth it. The blood and life essence were what she needed to keep herself rejuvenated and capable enough to rule. Once she stopped hearing rustling in her bedroom, Azazel decided it was time to get out of her bath.

She stood in front of the bathroom mirror and inspected every part of her body. Azazel was borderline giddy with the results. She looked like she had aged backwards and had a woman's body in her early twenties. Azazel smiled, relieved that her body finally looked the way she had been trying to make it look.

Walking out of the bathroom, she didn't bother covering herself up and was surprised when she saw Mulligan standing there, who automatically averted his eyes.

"Mulligan, announce yourself! You knew I was bathing!" Azazel walked across her room, still nude, not ashamed of her body.

Mulligan's gaze was locked on the floor as he said, "Yes,

Goddess, I apologize. I just wanted to inform you that the trash has been taken out."

This made Azazel scoff as she said, "Is that really any way to speak of the dead, Mulligan? Have some respect!"

Mulligan nodded. "Right, I'm sorry."

He took a deep breath. "The family began asking questions when I sent word for them to come to," he paused, "dinner."

Azazel smiled and walked toward him. She noticed how uncomfortable he was the closer she got to him. "You tell them nothing."

He nodded and replied, "Of course, Goddess."

Azazel nodded and turned away from him, dismissing him for the night. Before he left, she said nonchalantly, "I need a room with drainage. I want to make your job easy for you."

As she looked at the dark red stain on the floor, Mulligan cleared his throat and replied, "Leave it up to me, Goddess. I will find something. In the meantime, perhaps an area rug?"

Azazel nodded and continued to her closet, indicating to Mulligan that it was time for him to leave. As she walked in, she couldn't help but think of Mulligan's responses to her needs. She started to get irritated when she thought of him refusing to look at her like he was scared of her suddenly. And it wasn't even like he hadn't killed before!

It made no sense, and she felt she needed to get him back in line. Picking out a long silver silk nightgown, Azazel felt luxurious and tantalizing. Looking at herself in the mirror, she couldn't help but think about Antonio. But she had to push his face out of her mind. She had to focus on her dinner with the maid's family and the Cunning.

16

Azazel climbed into bed, and a smile crept across her face when she thought of drinking from the maid's neck. With a renewed sense of excitement, she looked forward to finding a new chamber to create the right atmosphere for her hunger. Staring into the darkness, she only saw the fear in her victim's eyes as she knew she was about to die. This brought Azazel an overwhelming sense of pleasure.

She lied in her bed and couldn't fall asleep for some time; instead, she thought of how the absorptions had changed over the years and her insatiable hunger.

Eventually, sleep consumed her, and Azazel didn't wake

up until the sun had set the following day. She kept seeing slides and chutes all leading to the same room in her dreams, a room she had never seen before. It was windowless and barren. Every time she was brought back to the room, she felt fear and hopelessness.

When Azazel opened her eyes, she had the most devilishly wicked idea. She sprung out of bed and didn't bother to change. She ran out into the hall and screamed, "Mulligan!" and walked back into her room, leaving the door open for Mulligan to arrive, which wasn't very long after Azazel had sat down on the couch. When he walked into the room, he nervously looked around as Azazel demanded, "Shut the door." He obliged and cautiously walked over to the couch to sit across from Azazel, who watched his every move.

She asked, "What's below this room?"

Mulligan's face scrunched up as he tried to remember and finally said, "It's empty, I believe."

Azazel nodded. "How long would it take to build a chamber?"

Mulligan's face scrunched again, and he looked at her in confusion before asking, "Chamber? Chamber for what?"

She sighed like she was bored. "Mulligan, I had an epiphany last night, and then the dreams that followed were so deliciously intricate and vivid. I want to build a chamber underneath my bedroom—windowless, bare, and a drainage system leading from it."

Azazel looked at Mulligan, who had a look on his face that resembled a mixture of curiosity and fear. She continued to her favorite part of the request. "I want there to be slides or chutes that lead to the room from this room, one way."

She stopped, and Mulligan looked around the room and asked, "Goddess, what is this room for?" he asked cautiously.

Azazel smiled devilishly and said, "Mulligan, I will make

your job even easier. Now, go find a contractor who will do the construction. Price isn't an issue, of course."

Mulligan cleared his throat and asked again, "Goddess, what if they ask what the room is for?"

She looked at him and said, "Just tell them it needs to be soundproof and discreet. If they ask any questions after that, find a new one."

Mulligan nodded, turned toward the door, and quietly asked, "Goddess, will you at least tell me what this room is going to be used for?"

"Clean up."

He nodded, clearly understanding, and left the room quickly.

After he left, Azazel stood up and walked into her bathroom; she decided she would have a bath and began to run the water. She walked over and picked out a jar of dried rose petals, lavender, and Epsom salts. She sprinkled the flowers and salts into the water when the tub was full.

Once she smelled the floral scent in the steam and got undressed, she lowered herself into the bath, letting out a sigh of relief as she leaned back and allowed herself to get used to the heat of the water and focus on the sweet-smelling flowers. She had cleared her mind of any thoughts and was basking in the silence until she heard heavy footsteps and a light knock, followed by Mulligan's voice yet again.

"Goddess?" Azazel groaned and shouted, "Come in, Mulligan!"

He came into the bathroom and averted his eyes. "Goddess, I have several contractors prepared to meet with you at your convenience."

Azazel opened one of her eyes and looked at her advisor, who was sheepishly standing in front of her. She groaned and snapped, "Oh, Mulligan. You've seen me nude before. Get a grip; you're pathetic."

He raised his eyes to meet hers. "I just believe in respecting you and your privacy."

They stared at each other in silence for a moment before she eventually said, "I will meet with them this afternoon before the maid's family." She smiled at him while Mulligan bowed slightly and removed himself from Azazel's presence.

Once he was gone, and she couldn't smell his stench any longer, Azazel returned to her world of relaxation and contemplated the future in her new absorption chamber.

When she felt good and clean, Azazel walked into her closet and knew the dress she wanted to wear. She pulled it out of its place and couldn't help but admire the beauty of the garment. It hugged her body and had lace decorating the back; there was no slip under the lace, and it barely hid her skin. She paired it with a pair of strappy neon pink stilettos and let her hair fall naturally around her body; when she did a final twirl in the mirror, she squealed in delight and left her room feeling invincible.

Mulligan was already waiting with five rough-looking men when she reached the dining hall.

Azazel smiled and said, "Gentlemen, welcome."

She walked over and shook their hands, and they all bowed with respect and nervously looked at Mulligan, who looked from them to Azazel. After they were all introduced, the man in the center, Thomas, stepped forward and asked, "Do you have plans?"

Azazel giggled and replied, "Oh, many, but physical plans, no. I just came up with the concept this morning. Walk with me, and I'll explain what I'm envisioning."

She led them all back to her chamber and waited for them to pile into her room, including Mulligan, before continuing with her idea.

"I envision a trap door somewhere behind the long couch over here." She motioned to where Mulligan had first found

Monica's body. "I'd then like a singular chute, approximately six feet by six feet, to drop about four feet before it separates into two different chutes. Both of those chutes will lead to a large cement room located under this room. I'd also like a drainage system to be installed."

This was when the red-headed man known as James interrupted her and asked, "Goddess—"

Azazel cut him off and said, "Wait until I'm finished," wagging her finger at him. She went on to say, "No windows. I'd like it painted stark white and tiled while also being soundproof. There is going to be one door that leads out that can only be unlocked from the outside."

The men all looked at each other, and James stuttered when he asked, "What is this room for?"

"Storage, of course!" She laughed, and the men nervously joined in.

Azazel stopped laughing and shouted, "Alright, can you begin today? Can this be completed this week?"

This caused the men to all begin laughing for real.

Azazel calmly said, "I will pay you any amount that you can come up with."

The tradesmen all exchanged looks and looked back at Mulligan, whose expression matched theirs.

The fallen angel continued. "Gentlemen, you have your plans, and I will leave it to you to delegate tasks, but you will be checking in with Mulligan if you have any questions as I have other obligations that need my attention. If you are not up to the task, please let him know, and we will find a way to handle the situation."

As she walked to the makeup room, Azazel was giddy; she always got such a rush over commanding a room of men like that. She found Dante leaning over the counter, putting the finishing touches on his own face. When he pulled away, Azazel was intrigued by his look. He gave himself silver glitter tears with a deep purple lip that caught the light so beautifully.

When he caught sight of her, he bowed. "Give me one second."

She held up her hands and sarcastically said, "Wouldn't want to interrupt your personal time."

Dante smacked his lips. "How do you expect me to make you look flawless if I can't even make myself look flawless?"

Azazel walked over to the chair behind him and sat down. He looked at her in the mirror and asked, "Where'd your sparkle go?"

"Lost its shine." She didn't even bother to look at him.

"You'll find it again. You always do."

Once he was done applying the last of his gloss, he turned to Azazel and asked, "Glam or natural?"

"Your call."

He began moving around her and applying different products onto her face. Azazel couldn't see anything he was doing, so she focused on bettering her mood for when she had to walk out into the public.

When Dante moved away from her to get the tools for her hair, Azazel was pleasantly surprised with what she saw. Everything was nude and very soft. It looked like she wasn't wearing any makeup at all, yet everything was enhanced and perfect.

When he finished, his leader had a look that screamed both sultry and sophisticated.

"Have I mentioned how much I like you?" she asked him, admiring herself in the mirror.

"You're welcome, Goddess."

17

When Azazel stepped out into the hallway, Mulligan rushed toward her and excitedly exclaimed, "They all agreed to the project!"

"Good, you're in charge, Mulligan. Don't let me down." She barely glanced at him before walking away.

"Goddess, maybe we should discuss the plans further?"

She stopped and looked at him. "Did you not hear everything I said earlier? I didn't realize you had suddenly turned deaf."

He turned flustered at her words. "Yes, I heard everything you requested, but I also had some thoughts that I think would benefit you as well."

"Continue."

Mulligan went on to explain a chute system that would dispose of her victims to an incinerator below, and an exhaust system to get rid of the smell. It would all be paired with a sprinkler system installed in the ceiling to help with the cleaning.

Azazel smiled and patted him on the shoulder. "That's much better." As she turned away from him, she had taken several steps before she called over her shoulder, "You're in charge, Mulligan! Make it good."

When she reached the front of the house, she saw Antonio walking up the stairs—in the same clothing he'd been in the night before. He tried to reach for her hand to kiss it, but she withheld it from him.

"Antonio," she said. She could see the hurt in his eyes. "Is there a reason you're here again?"

This caused Antonio to start apologizing for the night before and began begging for Azazel's forgiveness. When he was met with a stone-like response, he began to back away from her, and Azazel let him go. She watched him walk away and saw his shoulders hunch over; everything about him screamed defeated, and it made her feel victorious for a short while.

When Azazel couldn't see him anymore, she continued on her path into the town center. It was two days before the Cunning was set to happen, and Azazel could feel the buzz in the air as people whispered excitedly when she passed them.

She took her place on stage when she arrived and turned to face the crowd that had followed her, a solemn look on her face. "Deanna Morgan will no longer be competing in the Cunning. She and her family have been relocated. That is their contribution for this year's cycle."

The crowd around her began whispering amongst themselves. When Azazel looked out, she noticed members of the prominent families looking at each other in confusion, minus Antonio, who was only looking at her. Her voice caught in her throat as she continued, "The Cunning will continue as planned." She walked off the platform and pushed her way through the crowd to get away from them.

When she returned home, she walked past the dining hall, but was soon stopped when one of the servants asked, "Are you going to be eating this morning, Goddess?"

Azazel shook her head. "No, I'm planning on having a rather large dinner, so I won't be eating until then."

The servant bobbed up and down in a quick bow. Azazel continued to her chamber and found all the tradesmen in there. She looked at the workers for a short while before returning to the hall to call for a servant. A blonde man with kind green eyes came running to her, breathless.

"I will need to move into another large room until the renovations are done. Can you see if the master guest suite on the other side of the palace would be suitable for me?"

He nodded and took off running in the opposite direction. Azazel looked around her, realizing that there wasn't much for her to do until her guests came for dinner. She looked out the window to notice how beautiful the weather was and decided to stroll through the castle gardens. It had been ages since she stopped to smell the roses.

She walked through the back halls until she came to a short hallway that led out to the back of the palace. When she stepped outside, she was greeted by the scent of various flowers and different types of fragrant trees. As she walked through the rows of flowers, she couldn't help but imagine the possibilities with her new room. Azazel was pleased that the renovations were started so quickly, and she hoped the men would be so motivated by money that they got the job done even quicker than she had quoted them before.

She was so lost in her own thoughts that she didn't hear

the approaching figure until she almost ran into him. When Azazel looked up and saw Antonio's face, she stepped back.

"Antonio, I don't want to see you right now."

He looked at her and pleaded, "I can make up for last night. Please, let me make it up to you."

"It will take more than a little begging to make me forgive you, Antonio."

When she attempted to walk past him, he grabbed her arm and pulled her in for a passionate kiss. He put one hand firmly on her waist to hold her close to him and ran his other hand up to the side of her neck and face.

Azazel melted into his kiss and slowly wrapped her arms around his neck, pulling him closer to her. They lost themselves in the moment until she pulled back abruptly and said, "No, don't think you have some sort of... power over me, and that I'll just forget your behavior."

He took a step toward her. "I wasn't running from you, Azazel. I was running from how you made me feel in the moment." He looked at his hands and continued, "You made me feel vulnerable. I still don't know how to cope with that."

She took his hands and met his gaze. "Your heart is safe with me, Antonio."

"As is yours, Azazel."

She cleared her throat. "Well, I need to go back inside; there are a few things that I need to tend to."

Antonio nodded. "Yes, I should return home myself."

He looked at her and pulled her in for another kiss, longer and slower this time, full of unspoken promises. Azazel was the first to pull back, and she whispered, "Tonight, come when the palace has gone to sleep. I'll leave that door open for you." She pointed to the door that she had come out of. Antonio agreed and kissed her quickly one more time before prancing away.

Azazel watched him leave and felt her excitement soar. Walking toward the palace, her heart started to flutter. She had a smile on her face as she walked through the halls toward the guest chamber that she would take over during the renovation period. When she passed her bedroom and peeked in, she saw the furniture covered and moved to the other side of the room while the men were all standing around a large hole in the floor. Azazel was pleasantly surprised with their progress and continued on to her temporary chamber. Going to the other side of the palace seemed awkward to her as she rarely went over there, and the closer she got to the room, the quieter it got.

When she entered the guest room, she was pleased with how the room looked. Large bouquets of fresh flowers were put in every corner of the room, the windows were open, a pleasant soft breeze was coming in, and the earth-toned bedroom with the large four-poster bed promised comfort and hospitality during her stay. Azazel walked over to the closet, not sure what to expect. When she swung the doors open, she saw that it had been filled with a large selection of her clothing; she smiled. Her servants were on top of their tasks.

When she went into the bathroom, she was even more surprised to see that several body oils, containers of flowers, and different fragrances of salts were brought over. She felt grateful and considered for a moment to stop plucking the humans at her own discretion.

But she quickly pushed that thought aside. "They're just humans. Pathetic humans."

She placed the oil back in its place and continued with her inspection. When she was pleased with her surroundings, Azazel decided that she would go back to check in on the construction crew. Azazel slowly walked through the halls again and started to notice the small intricate designs on the pillars of the palace, the textures on the wall, and small details she had never cared about before.

The moment with Antonio in the garden came rushing back to her, and Azazel felt her face flush with embarrassment and smiled to herself; she knew tonight would be something extraordinary

As Azazel approached her bedroom, she heard shouting and arguing. This caused her to pick up her speed, and when she entered the room, they all went silent and exchanged looks with each other.

She smiled at them and asked, "Gentlemen, how are things going?" They all began talking at once, and she held her hands up. "One at a time, please."

Thomas stepped forward and said, "Mulligan told us that there needs to be enough support along the chutes to hold… a full-grown man…" He trailed off nervously.

"And… what's the problem?"

"We have no way of testing it." He looked down at his feet.

"Nonsense!" She pointed to each man in the room and said, "I see enough grown men in this room to ensure that the supports are sturdy enough for my plans." Thomas looked around the room and mumbled something, to which Azazel thundered, "What was that?!"

Thomas didn't hesitate. "I will not lose any men over whatever freakshow you have planned."

Azazel took a step toward him and placed a finger on his chest. It started to subtly glow as she said, "You will do whatever needs to be done."

"I will not," Thomas repeated, and the crew exchanged looks once more.

Azazel glared at them and demanded, "Is there anyone else who shares the same thoughts as Thomas?" They all shook their heads quickly. "Good, now let's get back to work. Quickly!"

They all dispersed and began tackling different tasks in the room as Azazel watched for a short while. When she was satisfied with their workflow, she left the room as Mulligan was rushing in to talk to the tradesmen.

When he saw that Azazel was in the room, he exclaimed, "Ah, good! Goddess, your dinner guests will be arriving soon. Would you like to change before entertaining them?"

Azazel nodded and replied, "Yes, Mulligan, thank you. Also, I'd like to dine with them in the far dining room, closer to my temporary chamber. If you wouldn't mind telling the chef that."

"I'll go to the kitchen right away and inform them!"

Azazel scanned the room once more and leaned in to whisper, "When they are done, I want them all locked in the room."

This caused Mulligan's face to whiten as he looked at her and repeated, "All of them?"

Azazel seethed. "Every. Single. One."

He looked out at the men, unknowingly building their tomb.

Azazel grinned, and before she left him standing there, said, "It's deliciously wicked to know what they are in for, isn't it?"

He didn't reply but simply looked to the floor, and Azazel was bored of toying with his conscience. She sauntered out of the room and strolled back toward the other side of the palace. The closer she got to her room, the more excited she became for the meal that was about to take place.

She smirked as she opened the door and walked in; she knew exactly the right dress to wear for the occasion. Azazel swung the doors of her room open and walked swiftly to the wardrobe to pull out a deep red dress. She looked at it and knew it was *perfect*. She hung it on the door and walked into the bathroom to begin a ceremonial bath.

Once the water had reached the right level with the perfect amounts of essential oils and salts, Azazel undressed and stepped into the tub. She immediately dipped her whole body under the water, and as it came up over her face, she took a deep breath and plunged herself into the sweet-smelling water. When she rose again, she was surrounded by the curtain of her hair. Pushing it to the side, Azazel leaned back against the tub, allowing her mind to be quiet as she enjoyed the moment.

She finally felt the urge to get out of the tub and lifted herself up. As she stepped out, her hair swept over her face again, and she was overtaken with the scent of sweet figs. Azazel smiled and was pleased with the smell that it had left on her skin. When she walked out of the bathroom, she grabbed the dress and slipped it over her head, careful to keep the material from touching her still wet hair. She stepped in front of the mirror, and her breath was taken away!

The shade of red resembled blood, and there was a fine golden glitter somehow embedded into the fabric, and was only visible if she turned a certain way in the light. It was floor-length, and while the bodice was tight, the skirt was flowy, and Azazel liked how it fanned out when she spun around.

She looked at herself in the mirror one last time and said, "At least if things get messy, it'll blend in."

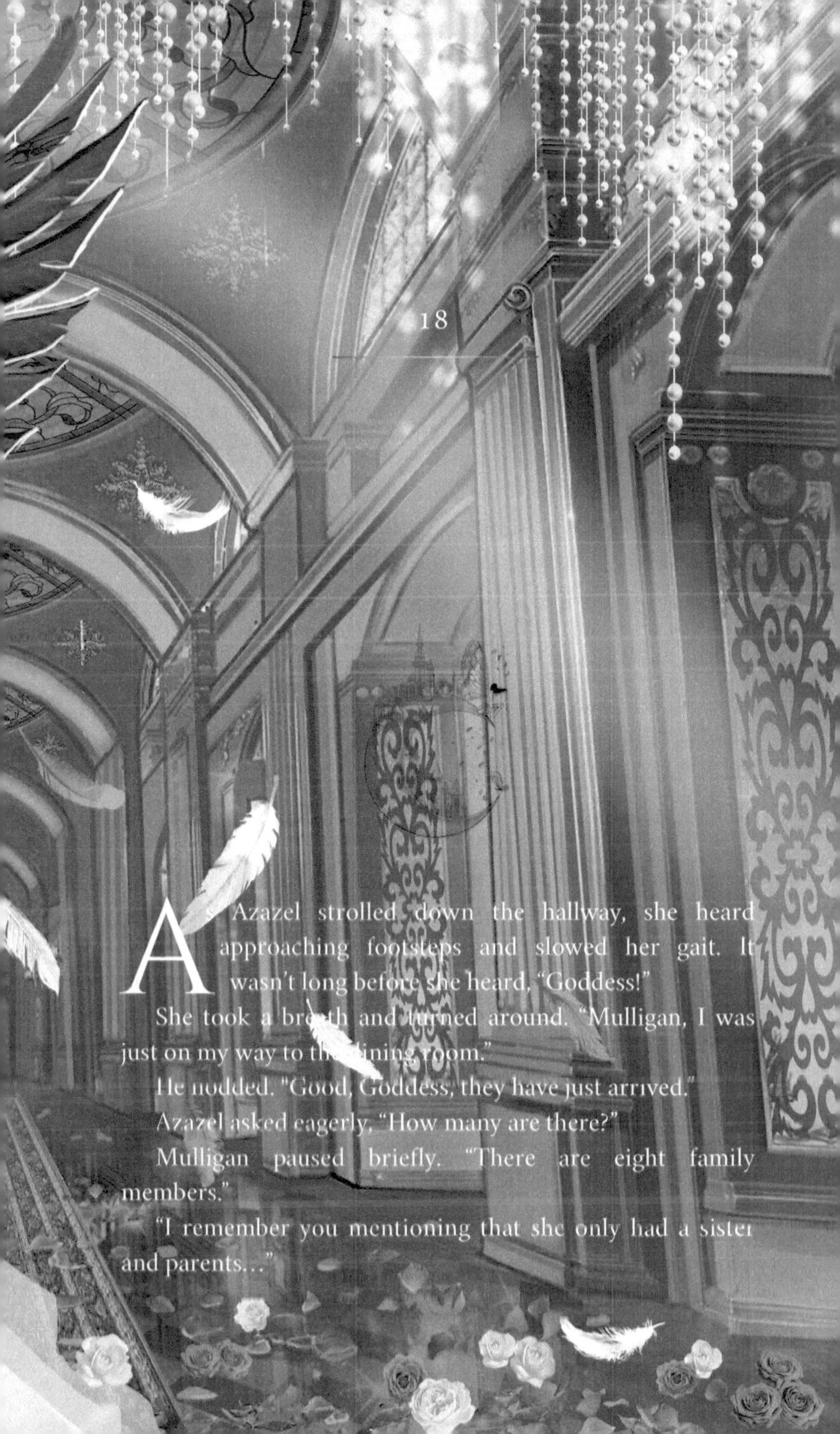

18

As Azazel strolled down the hallway, she heard approaching footsteps and slowed her gait. It wasn't long before she heard, "Goddess!"

She took a breath and turned around. "Mulligan, I was just on my way to the dining room."

He nodded. "Good, Goddess, they have just arrived."

Azazel asked eagerly, "How many are there?"

Mulligan paused briefly. "There are eight family members."

"I remember you mentioning that she only had a sister and parents…"

"Extended family was present when we went to the house. I thought it was a safe decision to bring them all here on your behalf."

Azazel smiled at him as she raised her hand to cup his cheek. "You did well, Mulligan. Thank you." She turned away from him and started to walk toward the dining room once again, with him following closely behind.

She could smell the desperation oozing from them when she reached the family. The maid's family watched her enter the room and dipped in low bows. When they all came up again, an older man stepped forward and introduced himself as the maid's father, Clarence. His wife, Catherine, introduced herself, and they all took turns saying their names. Azazel stopped listening once Catherine had stopped talking, but went through the motions of shaking each of their hands.

Once they had finished speaking, Azazel thanked them for coming and motioned to the table behind them. The family started talking about the maid's whereabouts, while Azazel watched them stuff their faces without taking any for herself. Bella, she found out her name was.

Azazel cleared her throat as she stood up and said, "You've probably all been wondering what I am going to do to help find Bella." They bobbed their heads and exchanged looks. "I am just going to get right to it. Bella isn't coming home. She's dead."

The family broke out in tears and started shrieking in distress. Azazel raised her voice, "There is no need for any of this; you'll all be joining her shortly."

Through tears, Catherine asked, "What? What do you mean?"

Azazel walked over to the sliding doors at the entrance and closed them, locked them, and turned back to the family, who began to panic. She grinned and walked over to the eldest family member, Beverly, who couldn't even stand on her own. Azazel picked her up by her neck and started to squeeze until she heard the crunch, and Beverly slumped over in her hand.

The family watched in horror, and all rushed to stand up and run toward Azazel, who scanned the room and flicked her finger at each one of them. This created an invisible wall that kept them from her, and when Clarence began to scream, nothing but a grunt came out of his mouth.

When Azazel looked at him, she asked, "Have you not figured it out yet? I am not human!"

She snapped her fingers, and his scream came out at full volume. She then looked at the rest of the family and snapped her fingers again, forcing them to stay planted where they were, regardless of how much they struggled.

She looked down at Clarence. "Just to make things easier." She plopped down on his stomach and slapped his chest; he grunted. "In ancient times, they used to sacrifice humans to the gods, sometimes without any numbing agents, and they would cut the victim's heart out while they were still conscious. They thought the fear strengthened the sacrifice."

Clarence started to grunt and move his eyes rapidly, and Azazel leaned forward and asked, "I can smell your fear. I can smell your family's fear. And do you want to know what it smells like?" Clarence just grunted. "I am going to assume that you want to know, so I will tell you. It smells delicious, like freshly-baked bread and warm butter."

She watched Clarence's eyes widen as she nodded encouragingly. "Yes, exactly! Hence, you see my dilemma regarding self-control." Azazel looked around the room and felt her mouth salivate. The hunger in her core had become too hard to ignore. The family watched her intensely, and she said, "I killed Bella. Her life essence rejuvenated me in a way that I haven't felt in decades." She smiled as the family started to grumble, and she could feel their anger.

"It was for *me*! It was to replenish *me*! All of you will still be with me and a part of me *forever*. Your essence is entangled with my divinity at a cellular level. It's a fairytale!" Clarence tried to move underneath her, and Azazel pressed against him even more. "Oh, Clarence, no."

As she inched up on top of his chest and started to squeeze the sides of his body with her thighs, she heard Clarence's muffled scream of pain. She shivered as she looked down at him.

"When humans feel pain, it feels like someone has poured water down my spine in the most delightful way." Clarence's eyes started to produce tears, and she whispered, "I imagine you're in immense pain right now. It's going to be over soon, I promise." She patted his cheek and got off of him, causing him to let out another muffled scream.

She walked around the room and roared, "I haven't had this much power in a very long time!" She stopped to stroke cousin Edward's cheek. "And tonight's a special treat for me. I'd only expected three of you to come, so I am indulging quite a bit tonight!"

She looked at the table and walked over to a large platter with a long knife. Azazel grabbed it and walked straight to Catherine. She grabbed her arm, made a long incision from her arm to her wrist, and watched in delight as blood flowed out like a fountain. Azazel brought Catherine's arm up to her mouth and began drinking deeply, letting it flow down her neck, saturating the front of her dress.

Catherine eventually fell to the floor, barely breathing. Azazel pushed her over so she was facing the ceiling and started to step on her lungs, and the family watched in horror, all of their screaming muffled.

Azazel looked down at Catherine and taunted her, "Come on, Catherine, you need to let go if you want to be reunited with sweet Bella."

With one final muffled grunt and a sigh, the orb started to float up from her mouth. The family continued to watch as Azazel dropped to her knees and wrapped her lips around the orb. Her skin started to glow, and she looked around the room and asked in a husky tone, "Okay, who's next?"

Azazel went through the entire family until the room was littered with their bodies. She slowly walked over to Clarence, who was trying to rock his body but grunted in pain every time he moved. She loomed over him, her neck and dress covered in his family's blood. He looked up at her with tear-filled eyes, and she dropped down to him.

"Oh, Clarence, did you think I forgot about you?" She leaned forward and kissed his forehead. "No, I would never!"

He began to sob softly. Azazel placed her hands on his chest and pressed down hard as her hands began to glow. She watched as he began to cave under the pressure of her divinity; she didn't have to wait long for his life essence orb to float up out of his mouth. Once she was finished, she stood up and looked around the room. Azazel sighed in relief, finally feeling complete.

She walked to the doors, and when she slid them open, Mulligan was waiting on the other side; he looked past her.

"Good meal?" he asked.

"It was satisfactory." When she turned to him, she asked, "How long do you think it's going to take for the chamber to finish building?"

He looked at her and replied, "They finished the chute to the incinerator today."

"You found an incinerator this quickly?"

Mulligan nodded and proudly responded, "I told them who it was for."

Azazel patted him on the back as she walked past him. "I need to go change, Mulligan."

She wasn't far from the room when she heard him gasp as he saw the severity of her evening.

19

When she arrived back to her room, Azazel felt satisfied and knew that nothing would interfere with her night with Antonio. Confidently, she went over to her wardrobe and pulled out a delicately strapped silver mini dress. After she cleaned her face and put the dress on, she loved how she could barely see her body underneath the material; she knew Antonio would have difficulty formulating words when he saw her.

Azazel wanted to see how far the workers got. However, the sun was beginning to set, and she knew she needed to run to her chamber. When she peeked around the corner and into the room, she was pleased to see that they were still working; the trap door had been installed.

Not wanting to disturb them, she tiptoed past the construction site. She wanted to grab a few things from her bedside table, and when she reached her destination, she pulled open the drawer and grabbed some oil in an intricate bottle. She quickly left the room before anyone saw her and waited for Antonio at the door, warming the bottle in between her hands.

As each moment passed, her heart started to race faster, and she began to worry that he wouldn't show up. Luckily, she heard the door start to open and was greeted by Antonio's handsome face.

They looked at each other and instantly rushed to one another. Antonio picked Azazel up and carried her as she whispered directions to her room in between kisses. When they got to her room, he put her down in front of the door, and she took him in by the hand. The night was filled with the most passionate touches and ecstasy.

Azazel watched the sun rise through the window the next morning as she rested her head on Antonio's chest. She contemplated this genuine feeling of happiness and smiled, knowing that she didn't have to use any of her divinity to sway Antonio to be here. He loved her, and she felt *herself* falling in love with *him*. She looked up at his face, noticing how long his eyelashes were and the small scar above his eyebrow; her gaze followed the defined lines of his body in admiration.

She watched him sleep for a few moments longer, and when she attempted to move, he woke up and sleepily grabbed her, pulling her back into him. They spent the morning rolling around in bed, exploring each other and deepening their connection.

Finally, Antonio wanted to grab some food. Azazel agreed

and told him she would have something waiting for him when he got back. He smirked while he got dressed and looked back at her. She watched him and playfully taunted him as he left the room. Azazel stepped out of bed and walked toward the bathroom to start a bath for the two of them. She remembered the bottle from the night before and grabbed it from the small entryway table. She was relieved to see that it wasn't knocked over in all the commotion. Azazel returned to the bathroom and took the stopper off of the bottle; the aroma that filled the air was sweet, seductive, and filled her senses with pleasure.

She put a few drops into the running water and watched the tub fill up. She then stopped it and stepped into the tub when it reached a suitable level. Azazel cupped water up over her shoulders and submerged her entire body into the depths of the tub. She didn't even hear Antonio creep in at first until he came looking for her.

He took the sight of her in and asked, "Should I just feed this to you?"

"No, you should join me, and we can share."

Antonio placed the platter on the counter beside him as he stripped down again before picking it back up, lifting it over his head as he stepped into the tub behind her.

Once he got settled and placed a strawberry into her mouth, he asked, "Mulligan was asking about you."

Azazel sighed. "Of course, he was. Did he say what he wanted?"

Antonio paused as he thought. "He mentioned construction."

This piqued Azazel's interest, and she didn't want to wait. She wrapped herself in a plush robe and left Antonio to clean up the mess and tidy up the room. Azazel walked quickly down the halls, and as she turned the final corner before her chamber, she noticed that it was quiet… too quiet.

She walked a bit faster and saw that her bedroom door was shut.

Azazel opened the door slowly, and everything had been put back and cleaned up. She walked into the room and looked around. She then heard a knock on the door and saw Mulligan come into the room, and he looked around before asking, "Are you ready to see it?"

"Is it ready?"

Mulligan nodded and turned to leave the room, Azazel following close behind.

He led her to the lower level of the palace, and as they approached the room, Azazel could smell fresh paint and wood. She took a deep breath in, and Mulligan stopped in front of her and said, "I made a few adjustments. I hope you don't mind."

Azazel tilted her head. Mulligan continued, "The trap door is run by a trigger pulley system. Your victim will walk over the door and hit the small hook sticking up from the floor, and then they will fall down the chute and into this room here."

He motioned to a large room built in the middle of the floor. Azazel looked above her at the chutes, and before she could ask, Mulligan spoke again, as if reading her mind. "It can hold up to four hundred pounds."

He went to unlock the door, which had a latched hook and padlock. When they stepped into the room, Azazel was filled with happiness. It looked identical to the room from her dream! It was pure white with a singular significant drain in the middle of the floor. There were no windows, and once the door was shut, they couldn't see the seam of the doorframe.

She looked around and asked, "Clean up?"

Mulligan answered, "Ah, yes, the best part."

He walked over to a section of the wall opposite them and

pushed it inwards. It shifted around and revealed another chute. Azazel walked over and looked down. "The craftsmanship is impeccable!"

Mulligan agreed. "It can be quickly washed. Sprinklers will drop down from the ceiling; there is a system for the water and another for cleaning detergents. I also made it soundproof except for a small part of the room, where you'll only be able to hear anything happening down here on *your* side of the bed."

Azazel took a step back. "Mulligan, every time I lose faith in you, you somehow find a way to blow my mind. Now, where are my lovely tradesmen?"

"Eating their last meal in the grand dining room. I figured it was the least we could do."

"Least *we* could do? Mulligan, I'm the one who benefits from them, not you." She rolled her eyes at him. "I want them all in here within the next hour!"

Mulligan nodded, and then he asked, "Will you be joining the final meal for the combatants?"

"Antonio and I will be down after the loose ends are tied up."

She left Mulligan looking around the new room. He was borderline uncomfortable that the room was being used so soon; Azazel could hear it in his voice. How weak. Humans were all so weak.

She pushed his facial expressions out of her mind as she returned to Antonio. She was excited to tell him that they could finally return to her regular chamber. That they'd have access to the finest clothing again... just in time for the final dinner.

They walked down the halls hand-in-hand; Azazel was happy, and Antonio seemed at ease with her. When they got to her chamber, she welcomed him in.

"Ah, it's good to be home." He playfully threw his arms

into the air. "So, what will you be wearing?" He turned around and asked her.

"This." She walked into her closet to pull out a white dress completely covered in jewels in a backless design, and strings of natural diamonds hung across the back. There was also a long slit on the side and long-fitted sleeves.

Antonio gawked at her. "Wow."

She smiled and hung it back up. When she walked back into her room, Antonio looked around and asked, "So, where was the construction?"

Azazel felt a lump form in her throat, and she quickly replied, "I just had some flooring replaced. I tried to move the couch, and I cracked the boards underneath it when I set it back down."

It was such a quick lie, but he seemed to have bought it. Hopefully, he'd never discover her secret and master plan.

20

A solid knock on the door soon interrupted them. Antonio got out of bed, wrapped one of the bedsheets around himself, and walked over to the door to allow the designer into the room. When the designer read the room, he flushed red.

"Would you like me to give you a moment?"

Azazel shook her head. "Nonsense, what did you bring?"

The designer turned back to his rack and started to bring out suits in various colors, materials, cuts, and even tried to pass off a short suit. Azazel crawled to the edge of the bed and watched as the designer, Gustav, started to pair colors to Antonio's eyes and skin tone.

She watched the two men consumed by their conversation and smirked. She stepped off the bed and cleared her throat. "Boys, I'm going to go get ready myself." She pointed at Gustav. "Make him look pretty."

Antonio smirked at her, and she winked in response before turning to go to the closet. Azazel took the dress out of its bag and walked into the makeup room, where Dante was waiting and filing his nails.

When he saw her, he gasped. "Your sparkle has become a glow!" Dante got out of the chair that he was sitting in and patted it, telling her to come sit.

When she sat in front of the mirror, Azazel's mouth dropped open at her reflection. Her hair looked full of luster and was *perfect*, while her skin was so smooth and shiny that she resembled a star!

Dante stared at her. "Whatever you're doing, keep doing it!"

Azazel smiled at him. "Okay, the Cunning dinner."

Dante nodded, glanced at the dress, and back to Azazel. "Gotcha, well, since you *are* wearing white, it already makes you look absolutely ethereal, and I don't want to disturb that." She started to frown, and he jumped in again. "But I'll do what I can to accentuate your features!"

"Maybe just the smallest bit of pampering, Dante."

He bowed and began a skincare regime, finishing it with a simple moisturizer and lightly-tinted lip balm. When he finished, they were shocked to see that her skin look even more supple and youthful than before! Dante finished by placing hot curlers all over her head, and while those dried, he painted her nails a midnight black.

When her hair was done, they looked at her in the mirror, and both of them were taken with emotion. Azazel was genuinely happy, and she whispered, "I am so beautiful!"

"You always are, Goddess, but there's something more here. Something you're not revealing."

She wasn't ready to get into details about Antonio yet, so she changed the topic. "Can you help me get into my dress?"

Dante smiled. "I would be honored."

Once she was dressed, Dante covered his mouth and slightly shook his head in disbelief. "You're perfect!"

She turned around slowly, causing the diamonds on the back of the dress to chime together.

He looked down at her feet and asked, "What are you going to do for shoes?"

Azazel looked down also and asked, "Would it be awful to go barefoot?

Dante laughed. "While I do love the natural look, I think this look requires at least a six-inch heel."

She left the makeup room feeling like she was on top of the world. As she approached her chamber, Mulligan rushed down the hall toward her. She looked at him and greeted him.

"Goddess, your earlier request has been fulfilled."

"Good, I hope there wasn't too much trouble."

Mulligan had a guilty look on his face. "I had to gas them and drag them into the room one by one."

"Mulligan, our relationship is such a rollercoaster; continue to keep me on my toes."

"Of course, Goddess." As he turned, Azazel stopped him.

"Can you ensure that everyone is completely out of the palace tonight?"

"The room is soundproof, Goddess. No one will hear you."

She leaned in and whispered, "I am going to put it to the absolute test."

"Do you hear them now?"

Azazel shook her head, but then her face turned serious. "But I probably would if I were in my chamber."

When she went back into her room, she was relieved to see that it was empty, but was also confused as to *why* it was empty. She tiptoed across the floor and stepped on the part that creaked. She then heard a muffled sound and turned her attention to where the bed was.

She slowly walked over to it, and the closer she got to the side that she slept on, the louder the screams were. Azazel could hear the desperation in their voices, and she could smell their fear through the vent. She stood there for a few moments, soaking in the feeling.

When she finally felt a slight tug of urgency, she continued to the wardrobe to pick out a pair of black strappy platforms. After she put them on, she checked her appearance one last time and walked back out to her bedroom... where she saw Antonio standing by the couch in front of the trap door. He was dressed in a deep blue velvet jacket with a black shirt and tie. She stopped to take him in; he whistled his approval at her look, and she did a slow turn for him. Azazel stepped toward him, and he met her halfway to kiss her.

When she pulled away, she said, "I wish we could just stay here instead."

Antonio smiled at her and tucked a piece of hair behind her ear. "I think we would get sick of the men screaming under us after a while."

She pushed him back slightly. "Pardon?"

"Why is there screaming coming from under your floor, Azazel?" His face was glowing red with anger.

She attempted to take a step toward him, and he held his hand up to stop her. "No, you stay away from me!"

Her heart started to break as she pleaded, "Antonio, I would never hurt you. Stop!"

He glared at her. "I don't know about that. How many men are down there?"

When she didn't reply, he whispered, "Oh my god…"

This caused Azazel's face to darken, and she hissed, *"Your* god? I am the closest thing you have to a god, the only god who has ever given you everything you have ever wanted!"

Antonio started to back away from her as she approached him, but she marched toward him, not taking her eyes off him. She felt her heart shattering; she could see the fear and judgment in his eyes. Even if she *did* erase his memory, she knew that he'd still think differently of her; it was no longer pure.

"Antonio, I'm not going to hurt you."

"I thought you loved me…" he trailed off, and Azazel rushed to him to grab his hands.

"Antonio, I do; you just have to trust me."

He stared into her eyes, and she could tell that he was genuinely thinking through everything. He dropped his hands, straightened his jacket, and said, "Let's go to dinner. I'll leave after."

"That's it?"

He nervously looked around and asked, "What else is there to say? Do I have a choice? It's either I keep my mouth shut, or I join the men in the basement."

She could hear the betrayal in his voice, and it saddened her. He didn't offer her his arm, but instead, walked away from her before she could say anything. Azazel followed him out of the room, and as they continued down the hallway, the angrier she got with him. By the time they reached the grand dining room, Azazel was fuming. She tried to put a smile on her face as people rushed up to her, but she watched Antonio walk over to Mulligan and whisper something in his ear. Mulligan looked at Azazel, and he had a questionable look.

She saw Antonio lean back and nod his head, and then Mulligan left the dining room.

Finally, Azazel shouted, "Please! Everyone, let's eat!"

The crowd broke up to go to their tables, chattering excitedly. Antonio took a seat with his family instead of at the high table with her. This hurt her even more, and she began to tap her fingers on the table as she saw him lean over and whisper something to his brother, who then looked at his cup and took a sip. When Antonio looked up and saw that Azazel was glaring at him, he nodded and motioned his eyes to the hallway. She got up when he did, and they walked out as the staff started to bring in dinner.

When the head chef walked past her, Azazel stopped him and asked, "Can you tell them to wait until I speak?"

She turned her attention to Antonio. "Have you been spreading lies?"

Antonio shook his head. "I just told Mulligan to let them go."

Azazel's vision turned hazy with rage, and she slowly asked, "You… what?!"

"I told Mulligan to let the men loose. They are to be paid handsomely, and none of them will say anything or blacklist the palace for future work."

He's joking! He must be joking!

21

"I know you're not serious right now."

Antonio took a deep breath. "No, I am."

"And your reason?"

He paused before he replied, "You're about to absorb ninety-nine combatants, Azazel. Isn't that enough for you?"

Azazel took a step back from him and whispered, "What?"

Antonio sighed and said, "My family has known for generations about the reasoning behind the Cunning. It was the main motivation for our success." Azazel couldn't believe what she was hearing, but he continued, "This was supposed to be a yearly sacrifice, and you're starting to eat more than your fill." He looked up at her to see how she was taking it; she stared at him in shock.

The hall was quiet, and Azazel finally said, "I can't talk about this now. I have a kingdom waiting for me to address them."

Antonio grabbed her arm and asked, "Aren't you curious about what we know?"

She seethed in a hushed tone. "I don't care, Antonio."

He took a step back from her and bowed slightly. "I will be sure to stay out of your sight, Goddess." Antonio didn't bother looking up when he turned away from her. Azazel watched him walk away and felt a pang of fear start to creep up inside of her.

If humans found out what she was genuinely doing, there was no telling *what* they would try to do to her.

She collected herself again before she walked back into the hall. As she walked across the front of the room, she tried to push Antonio out of her mind. Azazel refused to let a mortal man have any sort of control over her emotions; she was done with him and would focus on her kingdom once again.

As she stood in front of everyone, they erupted into thunderous applause, and Azazel felt loved. She held her arms up to show them that she was appreciative of their support. She motioned to the combatants, which caused the dining hall to go wild with excitement. The combatants all stood up and waved to everyone cheering them on.

Once the murmuring had died down, Azazel thundered, "Everyone, eat as if this is your last meal!"

There was a ripple of laughter throughout the crowd as people started to fill their plates. Azazel waited for everyone to begin eating before she walked back out into the hall; she wanted to find Mulligan.

And as if he had known that she was thinking of him,

Mulligan turned the corner, and when he saw her, he stopped in his place. She rushed toward him and slapped him across the face when she reached him—the sound echoed through the hall, and a hot red mark was left on his cheek.

She leaned in close to him and hissed, "How dare you take orders from someone else?" Mulligan opened his mouth to speak. "Shut up! I'm speaking!" He nodded, and she continued. "No one takes orders from Antonio, and it startles me that he got so comfortable in my palace, with *my* servants so quickly."

"Goddess, my apologies, but Antonio claimed that those were your orders."

Azazel rolled her eyes and replied, "Mulligan, use your stupid brain. Do you really think I would ask you to do that?"

"I had hope, Goddess. The men had done such a great job. I personally felt like they deserved to keep their lives."

Azazel sighed. "Are they gone?"

Mulligan nodded.

"You're sure they won't say anything to anyone?"

Mulligan nodded again. "Antonio said he would triple whatever you were paying them to keep quiet, and still continue work when needed at the palace. At first, the men objected, understandably, but when I threatened to leave them there for you, they were more than agreeable."

"Ah, a happily-ever-after ending for everyone then, isn't it?" she declared sarcastically.

Mulligan asked nervously, "What do you want me to do about Antonio?"

"He's my problem. You leave him to me."

"I know it's not my place, Goddess, but I like how happy you are when you're with him. Please, go easy on him."

She paused for a moment. "You're right, Mulligan. It's *not* your place. You can stay out of my sight for the rest of the night."

Mulligan bowed again and left Azazel, who was trying to control her rage. She needed to take a moment to compose herself before she went back into the dining hall, and when she walked into the room, the atmosphere was light and full of happiness. It made it easier for Azazel to push her anger to the side; for the time being, she wanted to focus entirely on the combatants and their last night. She made her way through the aisles between the tables, talking to random citizens briefly before walking to the high table and taking her place in the center.

Azazel sat down and watched the crowd as they ate their meals; the combatants talked amongst themselves and ate as much as possible. She could feel the power radiating from the combatants' table in large waves. It made her mouth salivate, and she couldn't stare at them for too long, or the hunger would take over, and she wouldn't be able to stop it.

She stood up as people started to leave the hall, and she walked over to the combatants, who were all waiting patiently for their instructions.

"Hello, my strong warriors. After all of your hard work and training, we are finally on the eve of the Cunning." The combatants all straightened up with pride. She continued, "I expect you all to get to bed early tonight and meet at the atrium tomorrow morning, bright and early!"

She smiled warmly at the table, who all exchanged looks of uncertainty. Azazel closed her speech out by thanking them again for their sacrifice. When she turned to walk away from the table, she heard them all start to whisper.

She whipped herself around quickly and asked, "I'm sorry? Did someone have a question?"

When no one answered or raised their hand, Azazel turned to leave again. This time, it was the silence that haunted her as she left them, and it was deafening!

This evening had been filled with so much disappointment, and she didn't know how she would get past the feeling of being let down. Azazel grabbed the doorknob of her room and briefly wished that Antonio would be waiting for her inside. When she saw that the space was empty, she was slightly disappointed that the one order he listened to was the one where she told him to leave her alone. She sighed and continued to her closet to get changed for bed. When she looked around at all of the delicate sleepwear that she would have worn for Antonio, sadness started to creep in again. They had such a strong connection. What went wrong?

She walked over to her bed, but this time, she didn't hear screaming coming from her new chamber, and Azazel's sadness was replaced with anger again. She climbed into bed and pulled the bedsheets over herself; she hated feeling this way. She was of divine descent, and she *refused* to let a mortal have this much control over her. She knew having a consort would complicate things eventually.

Azazel's last thought before closing her eyes, welcoming sleep, was that mortals are best to be used and disposed of.

22

When Azazel opened her eyes the following day, she was filled with happiness and excitement. It was the day of the Cunning! She jumped out of bed and looked out the window; the sun was barely in the sky, and it was the perfect time for her ritual bath. She rushed into the bathroom and started the water, then she walked over to the cabinet and pulled out several bottles filled with clear liquid. She took the stopper out and dropped a few drops of each into the tub, chanting an incantation from an old language over it. She welcomed abundance and love into her life and wished the combatants a safe journey to the other side.

Once the water was done running, Azazel undressed and stepped into the tub. When she lowered herself fully into the water, she let out a small sigh of pleasure. She had gotten used to having someone with her consistently, and she almost forgot how nice it was to be alone. When she leaned her head back against the bathtub rim, images of her nights with Antonio rushed through her mind, causing her to sit up straight. Why did he keep popping up into her mind? She was done with him! That was that! She had better things to focus on.

The water was still warm when Azazel decided to get out of the bathtub. She knew it would take a while to get ready and wanted to put a lot of effort into her look. She walked to the end of the closet, where a long black gown was waiting for her. Azazel only wore it for the Cunning; it was made of the finest silk, and the seamstress who made it lost a large amount of blood sewing the rubies into it. Azazel would put the dress on and feel the dedication that the woman put into the gown.

She brought the gown with her when she went into the makeup room; she liked how useful Dante had proved himself to be when it came to getting her dressed. When she walked in, Dante already had his makeup done and was dressed in a smart plum-colored suit.

When he saw her, he ran over, took the gown from her, and rushed her into the chair as he said, "You're late!"

"Dante, I am never late. You're on my schedule, not the other way around."

Dante paused like he was going to say something, but then thought better of it and kept his mouth shut. They didn't speak while he got her ready, and Azazel didn't mind; she enjoyed the silence. When Dante was done with her look, she was pleased. He opted for subtle eyeshadow and long fake eyelashes with a nude lip and a bit of blush. Her hair had been straightened and was flowing around her. It was *perfect*.

Dante helped her into her gown and laced the back for her while she watched the look come together in the mirror.

"You know, Goddess, you don't have to hold this thing. Someone else can take over for once."

Azazel patted his hand and replied, "That's where you're wrong."

Dante had a confused look on his face but didn't say anything more. Azazel thanked him and told him that she expected to see him at the opening ceremony. She left him in a bowing position as she turned her focus on the Cunning, at last. She walked through the halls, smiling at servants that she passed, and as she was about to leave the palace, Mulligan ran after her, calling for her to stop.

When she turned around, Mulligan asked, "Did you need an escort to the atrium?"

Azazel rolled her eyes. "I guess I have no other choice, do I?" He offered her an arm. As she took it, she said, "I don't want you to say a word to me the entire way, Mulligan."

He made a motion across his mouth with his hand as if he were zipping his lips, and the two of them continued walking out of the palace. The streets were lined with flowers, and people were coming out of their shops to see her walk through the streets. Azazel smiled and acknowledged as many people as she could as she walked past them.

When they reached the atrium, a large crowd followed them into the building. The high families were all waiting at the shrine just inside the door. Azazel noticed that Antonio was nowhere to be seen; it was probably for the best. Mulligan let Azazel walk ahead to the families to welcome them as he went to double-check with the new staff that everything was ready.

The families warmly welcomed Azazel, all commenting

on how beautiful she looked and how excited they were to be there. She tried to keep her focus on the people talking to her, but she couldn't help but steal glances at the front door, hoping that Antonio would walk through it. But the closer they got to the opening ceremony, the clearer it became that he wasn't going to come.

A loud bell sounded, signaling that it was time to begin. The families all put on black robes and masks—each mask was an intricately carved animal face and painted black. They all formed a line behind Azazel and followed her out into the arena of the atrium. The family's duty was to bring the losing combatant of each round out of the stadium and into the back room, where she would be waiting at the end of every event to welcome the combatant to the next phase of their existence.

As they walked into the center of the arena, the families spread out behind Azazel, taking up the entire width of the stadium. Across from them, were the rows of combatants in their fighting gear, and they all had a weapon in their hands. Azazel looked out into the stands, where the kingdom had poured into the seats and were all excitedly talking. She put her hand up to her mouth and sounded off an ear-splitting whistle, which caused everyone to quiet down and focus on her.

"Welcome, everyone, to our millennium-old tradition, the Cunning!" The crowd didn't burst into applause. Azazel continued, "The combatants will be taking part in their final training session this morning, and then the events will commence this afternoon." The crowd started talking more, and she looked out at the masses, proud of what she had created in her world.

A woman in a hawk mask leaned over to her and asked, "Is there anything we can help you with, Goddess?"

Azazel turned her head slightly to the woman. "Have you seen Antonio?"

The hawk shook her head and replied, "Not since yesterday, Goddess. I'm sorry."

Azazel sighed and turned her attention back to the crowd; some were settling in their seats while others were starting to leave the arena.

The combatants all began to pair up again and went through stretches and basic moves. The families all dispersed and went to different parts of the atrium, some pairing up and others going off solo. Azazel wanted to find Antonio; she tried to put this to rest so that she could enjoy her absorptions like she usually did.

She started to walk out of the arena when Mulligan caught up to her and asked, "Goddess, are you not going to stay?"

Azazel shook her head and replied, "I'd like to find Antonio; I need to speak with him."

Mulligan looked down to the floor. Azazel studied his face and asked, "What is it, Mulligan?"

He quietly said, "He's in the chamber."

"What do you mean?!"

Mulligan refused to look up at her as he began to tell her that he drugged Antonio when they had a drink the night before.

She interrupted him to ask, "Why didn't I hear him screaming today, then?"

Mulligan said, "I think I gave him too much."

Azazel felt her heart drop, and she whispered, "You gave him too much of what?!"

"The liquid in your nightstand."

Azazel's mouth dropped. "How much did you give him, Mulligan?"

He began to speak quickly about how Antonio wasn't

worthy of Azazel, and that he was angry about Antonio giving him commands and lying to him.

She reached out to Mulligan as she softly said, "I understand, but it was not your mess to clean up."

He nodded and said, "I'm sorry, Goddess. I just wanted to be in your good graces once more."

"I'm only hard on you, Mulligan, because I know what you're capable of. I know you're human, and you're bound to slip, but you have nothing to worry about. Did you check on him? Is he alive? Is he able to get up?"

Mulligan nodded, and Azazel rushed out the door and toward her palace.

She ignored all of the citizens that called after her as she ran past them, pushing her legs to go faster. When she reached the room in the basement, she could hear Antonio yelling from inside. She opened the door, and he quickly backed away, screaming for her to stay away from him.

Azazel walked into the room slowly, looked around, and asked, "You don't like it here?" Antonio panicked and screamed again; Azazel shushed him and said, "Antonio, no one can hear you. It's just us in here." She watched for a bit as he tried to look around the room for an escape. "You know, I was really starting to fall in love with you."

"I *did* love you, Azazel! I've loved you since I was just a young man!" Azazel was taken back. She reached out for him, but he recoiled and roared, "No! You let me out of here, now!"

But she only shook her head. "Antonio, I had every intention of letting you go and having a rational conversation with you. Your reaction, however, has shown me that you're not capable of that."

"Capable?! I'm locked in a box!"

"True, but if you hadn't been so quick to judge me, you'd probably be in the arena right now instead of begging me to let you out of here." Antonio dropped to his knees and shuffled over to her, and he started to beg for his life. Azazel looked at him and sneered, "This is incredibly unbecoming of you, Antonio."

He stood up and grabbed her arm. "Then tell me what I need to do to convince you to let me go."

"It's not that simple; you broke my heart. You've disappointed me more than once. I really don't think I can let you keep strolling around the kingdom like you do."

He dropped his hand and asked, "What do you mean?"

Azazel backed away from him and started to walk around the room's perimeter, trailing her fingers along the wall and refusing to look at Antonio. He watched her for a second before he asked again, "Azazel, what do you mean?"

She stopped when she felt a small latch. She pulled it, and a long shelf appeared out of the wall when a part of it moved back, and behind it, was an array of weapons.

Azazel giggled and finally looked at Antonio. "I didn't even know those were there."

Antonio rushed toward her, but she grabbed a long-serrated hunting knife, and he stopped as the tip of it touched his chest.

When he looked up at her, she wasn't the being whom he had loved for the better part of his adult life; it was a dark skeletal version of her. Azazel's mouth was drawn tight, and her eyes were completely white.

He pulled back, and she whined, "Oh, come on! You were just so confident; don't stop now!"

"W-what are you?"

She grinned a devious smile. "One of the fallen."

She lunged to knock him on his back and straddled his chest, and while he struggled against her, she started to apply her divine weight to hold him in place.

He stopped struggling and looked up. "Azazel! Stop it!"

"You'll be a part of me forever, Antonio. We'll be together forever."

When he tried to object, she plunged the knife straight into his chest, and his eyes widened when he realized what she had done.

He grunted as she pulled it out. She then shifted her body down his before leaning in to kiss him on the lips. Azazel began to softly sob as she kissed him. When she pulled back from him, the orb followed her lips, and she felt Antonio's body go limp. She cried out in pain as she felt the weight of her choice and rushed to his body as she absorbed his essence, kissing all over his face.

Azazel hugged his body and wept until she couldn't cry anymore. She heard a faint knock, and she yelled, "Yes?!"

Mulligan appeared in the chamber and saw what she had done. He looked at her and said, "I didn't intend for you to kill him."

She looked at Antonio's face and replied, "I didn't mean to kill him. He just… he became a liability." They were silent for a few moments before she said, "Leave him. I want a proper burial for him."

Mulligan watched as Azazel stood up and walked over to give him the knife.

She looked back at the room and said, "I liked that hidden cupboard, nice touch."

Mulligan bowed. "You are requested to appear at the atrium."

She held her hand up and waved, acknowledging him as she walked away from him. When she thought of Antonio's absorption, she felt an overwhelming sense of loss and stopped in the hallway as she collapsed to the floor, clutching herself. She kept seeing Antonio's eyes as he realized that she had stabbed him, and she felt her heart break every time.

And to make it worse, she didn't feel the rejuvenation from his absorption. She looked down the hall in front of her and knew people would be sent to find her if she didn't keep going.

Azazel pulled herself together and continued to the main floor of the palace. As she came into the public's view, she put a smile on her face and tried to forget about Antonio in the basement. She walked up to the large spectator's box that overlooked the entire arena when she reached the atrium. The crowd started cheering for her as she sat down on her throne. She was so overwhelm with a sense of love and relief that she concluded she didn't need a single person to bring her happiness. She had a kingdom filled with people who loved her no matter what, and none of them would ever find out about her true nature. Azazel wouldn't let anyone else get as close as Antonio had gotten; he was a fluke.

A loud siren sounded, and Azazel started to get increasingly excited. The combatants stopped fighting, and all fell into a straight line as the trainer came out from a side door. He walked across the arena and gave his last words of advice to each combatant. The crowd watched as the trainer finished going through the lines of combatants, and he took a step back, saluted them, and turned to Azazel, nodding; it was time.

She stood up and looked out into the darkness of the arena as it quieted down, and she simply said, "Fight hard, strike true," and blew a kiss out to the combatants. "Thank you for your sacrifice."

The hooded families came out from the sides of the atrium with bags of supplies for the combatants; as each warrior opened up the bag, Azazel started to get an idea of who would go far and who wouldn't just by their facial expressions. When all of the bags had been handed out, the floor of the atrium slowly dropped down to a subterranean arena that stretched out underneath the entire kingdom.

The stands and spectator's box were dropped down just under the atrium's main building, down into the harshest terrain; the spectators were all protected from the elements, thanks to the encasement around the stands. They found themselves in a thick forest with the temperature dropping, and Azazel watched as the combatants all exchanged looks as they paused, wondering where they should start.

A girl began to dig into her bag to pull out a thick jacket and long knife, and before anyone could move toward her, she ran off into the forest.

The other combatants followed her lead and put on warmer layers of clothing before running off into the brush. Azazel was disappointed that no one took advantage of the time to get the first kill in. She tried to focus her eyes on all of the warriors and didn't need to wait long as they began to light fires throughout the forest. She smiled, knowing that the first night's challenge was usually the deadliest; she looked forward to what could happen in the following hours.

Azazel was grateful that she was alone; she didn't want to have to put on a fake appearance for anyone at the moment. She also didn't know how she was going to break the news to Antonio's family. But she knew that it would have to be sooner rather than later; she sighed when she thought about the funeral for him. Her eyes started to well up with tears when she thought of Antonio's face, smile, and touch, and her heart began to break. For the first time, she felt true guilt about her absorption.

She remembered the look of judgment in Antonio's eyes when he found out her secret. She remembered how he had let his ego dictate how he reacted when she pushed him off her and how comfortable he'd gotten, enough to dictate orders to her staff and lie on her behalf. Thinking about this,

Azazel became angry almost immediately again; he deserved it! And now, he would be a part of her forever! She would never have to worry about him disappointing her ever again.

Azazel stood up and walked toward the combatants' final destination to wait for the incoming morsels. As she walked to the backroom, her excitement peaked, and she started to slightly skip down the last hallway.

When she walked into the room, she saw three combatants barely moving on stretchers, with masked family members standing to the side of the room.

Azazel dismissed them, and when they left, she quietly said, "Okay, little birds. I need you to let go."

They had fought so hard and had already been through so much that she didn't want to traumatize them as they left this existence. Azazel continued to walk around them and whisper sweet things to them, wanting them to naturally *want* to leave this world. During her third round around the room, one of the boys started to wheeze, and Azazel walked over to him. She heard him struggling to breathe, and she leaned down over him to kiss his forehead. As she placed her lips to his head, the orb started to poke through his lips. She smiled and knew he was waiting for her to come to him. She ingested the orb and kissed his head once more before continuing her journey around the room.

Once the other two combatants had given up their orbs, Azazel covered the bodies and whispered a short blessing over them before she left the room. As she exited, the hall was lined with several members of the high families, and none of them said anything as she walked past. Azazel wondered if they had somehow found out about Antonio; none of them bowed or made eye contact with her.

She started to get nervous, and when she saw Mulligan at the end of the hall, she began to walk a bit faster until she reached him.

He smiled at her and asked, "Having a good harvest?"

"Mulligan, did you tell Antonio's family about his death?"

He shook his head and replied, "I had figured you would want to handle that, Goddess. I left it up to you."

Azazel let out a loud sigh and walked away from him. Her paranoia was starting to get to her once again. She shook her head and focused back on the lush green forest below her as it came into view once again.

When she sat down on her throne, she felt a rush of electricity shoot through her body. The latest absorptions had taken effect, and Azazel felt energized. It felt like her adrenaline had taken over her! Her heart was pounding, and she leaned forward in her seat, eager to see a fight.

She scanned the forest below her like a hawk looking for prey, and after a minute, she finally found two combatants fighting in a clearing. It was an older man with salt and pepper hair against a petite blonde woman with her hair braided in two. Azazel watched as the woman blocked every attack and quickly dodged under her opponent's legs, and then crawled up his back to wrap her legs around his neck to snap it. The spectators watched as a white vehicle crisscrossed through the forest to the latest casualty; the woman had already run off into the trees.

Azazel was still riding on a high from her last absorptions. She motioned for the closest staff member to come closer, and when a young man with black hair and bright green eyes came forward, Azazel said, "I'd like you to go tell Mulligan that I'd like the fallen to be put on ice until I say otherwise, please."

The servant bowed and quickly ran out of the box. At the same time, Azazel turned her attention back to the forest, looking for more fallen warriors. But when she couldn't find any, she concluded that maybe they were just getting adjusted. She pouted for a brief moment before deciding that she would go back to the palace to start planning Antonio's funeral, so that when she told his family, she would have the plans all set for them. She still didn't know how she would tell them, but she figured that no matter how they acted, she could always give them a small touch and change their minds.

When she thought of Antonio again, her pain had already died down substantially. Azazel was comforted once more, knowing that he would always be with her, and she was going to plan the most beautiful funeral to show his family just how much he was appreciated in the kingdom.

As she was about to walk out of the atrium, one of the family members came running after her, wearing a fox mask. When she lifted the mask, Azazel saw that it was Antonio's mother, and she felt the pit in her stomach harden once more when the mother asked, "Goddess, have you seen Antonio?"

Azazel sighed and placed her hand gently on the woman's shoulder, and when she saw her fingers start to subtly glow, she quietly mumbled, "Antonio won't be coming back; he's dead."

She watched as his mother's eyes widened, and she asked, "What do you mean?"

Azazel looked her in the eyes. "There was an accident in the palace. He was injured when overseeing the renovations in my chamber; he passed almost immediately."

She lifted her hand from the old woman's shoulder as she watched her process the news.

"Oh, alright. Thank you for telling me, Goddess."

"I'm sorry for your loss."

She pulled Antonio's mother in for a hug, and before parting ways, she whispered, "I promise I will take care of you and your family."

The woman nodded and walked away from Azazel.

Azazel continued to watch the woman until she was completely inside the arena once more. When she thought of how the woman looked at her—and even though she was helping her cope with her touch—Azazel still saw the hint of sadness in her eyes. She genuinely wanted the family to heal and move forward with their lives; she would make sure that they felt everything they needed to so they could get through their grieving period.

As the palace came into view, she decided she would have the funeral in the flower garden, and have all the flower arrangements come from the palace grounds. When she saw the first servant available, she requested that the maid gather several other servants and start putting together elaborate arrangements for Antonio. When the maid gasped at the news, Azazel quickly told her to carry on with her orders as Azazel walked past her to go into the kitchen to request a special meal for the funeral luncheon. She was shocked to see that only the chef was in there.

When the chef saw her, he straightened up and attempted to make it look like he was busy. She held her hand up and said, "There will be no need for that. I am here because I am going to need a special lunch made for Antonio's funeral; it is planned for the day the Cunning ends. I want you to contact his family to find out his favorite meals. I want it as personal as possible."

The chef bowed quickly and replied, "Yes, Goddess. "

Azazel nodded at him and turned to leave the kitchen. She was almost run over by several other maids with arms full of flowers running past her.

And when she got back to her room, she closed the door behind her. The air felt heavy in the room, like it was missing something. She continued into the wardrobe and caught a glimpse of her reflection in the mirror. She was still wearing

Antonio's necklace. It had become so much of her that she had forgotten to take it off.

She touched the necklace and felt overwhelmed with a sense of pure, radiant love. This caused Azazel to crumble with emotion onto the floor. She felt like her lungs had collapsed, and the sounds coming out of her resembled meek shrieks of grief. As hard as she tried to push him out of her head, Azazel loved Antonio, and not having him around anymore would hurt for a long time.

She wasn't sure how long she sat on the floor and cried over the sweet moments with him. She was angry that she didn't think about her choice rationally before she killed him; it was like she was starting to lose control over her hunger.

Eventually, she heard a knock on the door. She sighed as she heard the footsteps approach; she knew exactly who it was.

She yelled out, "In the closet, Mulligan!"

Mulligan poked his head into the closet and said, "Goddess, you're requested at the atrium. They are running out of space in the freezer."

Before she could reply or even think, she was walking out of the closet; she suddenly felt like she hadn't eaten in a millennium. Her body felt deprived, aching, and desperate while her emotions over Antonio had stopped completely; she wanted—no, needed—to feed.

24

Mulligan followed Azazel out of the room, and while he was speaking to her, she heard none of it. She smelled death, and she only wanted to follow the sweet-scented trail in front of her. As she walked through the streets, a few people witnessed Azazel's eyes go white, and her cheeks started to sink in while her usually curvaceous body withered away to nothing but a skin-covered skeleton. As they recoiled in horror, Mulligan looked out at the people, who all ran away from her. He sighed, knowing they were about to approach a tipping point in Azazel's divine cycle. She was entering a phase where she was no longer able to keep the kingdom in the dark about her needs.

He had seen her enter this phase twice since he'd started working at the palace. It was always terrifying, and she was usually able to pull herself back from the brink of insanity, but this year seemed different. *She* was different. He didn't think she would ever *kill* Antonio, and now they were planning a funeral for him!

As they got closer to the atrium, Azazel started to run toward it, a low growl coming from the depth of her throat that sounded like thunder in the distance. Mulligan stopped before they got to the arena door; he hated seeing her go through the absorption process. He looked around as the spectators came out and watched the fallen angel in shock. Damage control *must* be done.

While Mulligan tried to calm the humans down, Azazel ran through the halls until she reached the giant walk-in freezer, close to the combatants' sleeping quarters. Upon opening the large sliding door, she saw forty bodies waiting for her, and she rushed inside.

One by one, she quickly snapped each of their necks; the sound of each one giving way was comparable to an appetizer. She began to walk around, waiting for the glorious moment, but she didn't have to wait long. Almost as if they were drawn to her, the life essence orbs started to all float up out of the combatants' bodies and lingered in the air before they could go any further. Azazel opened her mouth wide, dislocating her jaw, and started to inhale with such a force that all of the orbs from around the freezer were brought in to her inhalation vortex, and she absorbed them all at once.

She shuddered as her body began to fill out once more, and her curves returned. Her hair was once again luxurious and silky, and the last bits of the rejuvenation process started to take effect. Once she felt complete, Azazel looked around and said, "Thank you for your sacrifice."

She turned to step over a body lying behind her to leave the freezer. When she came back out, several staff members had blank, distant looks on their faces as they watched her walk past them.

Before she turned the corner, Azazel called out, "You're going to need a mop and a lot of bleach!"

Azazel walked out of the atrium and saw Mulligan in a seemingly intense conversation with some of the citizens, who all looked quite frightened when they saw her approaching. They bowed and quickly stepped away from her as she got closer to Mulligan.

When he turned around to greet her, she asked, "Where are they going, Mulligan?"

He looked over his shoulder, and then said, "Oh, they just wanted to get back to the Cunning."

"And we are still scheduled to have Antonio's funeral in the garden tomorrow?"

Mulligan looked sad as he nodded slowly and replied, "Yes, Goddess."

"Mulligan, smile! Antonio would have loved that everyone's attention is on him."

"Antonio would have rather been alive, Goddess…"

This caused Azazel to whirl around and rush back toward him threateningly as she seethed, "Antonio is lucky that I didn't just leave him for you to throw away like last night's trash. He's closer to me than any human will ever understand until the end of time. Trust me when I tell you that it's an honor for Antonio to be where he is right now, and I suggest you change your tone."

"Yes, Goddess."

Azazel stared at him for a moment before she started to walk back to the palace. Mulligan chose to hang around and attempt more damage control in the kingdom. She stormed through the hallways, fuming over Mulligan's audacity! Servants jumped out of her way as she marched through the corridors until she reached the back door leading to the garden.

As she stepped down onto the deck to open the door, the memory of Antonio meeting her there flashing in her mind, she paused as she grabbed onto the doorknob. She expected herself to crumble like before; when nothing happened, she shrugged and walked out to see numerous extravagant bouquets of blooming flowers placed all around the garden, with a large portrait of Antonio in the middle.

The closer she walked toward the portrait, the more love she felt, no longer carrying the guilt of killing someone she loved. Azazel knew that if Antonio truly loved her, he would be excited, happy even, to be a part of her. He really *was* in a better place, and Azazel felt like Mulligan didn't know what he was talking about. He would *never* know what she felt.

She stared at the portrait and was overwhelmed with gratitude for their time together and the things he showed her. Azazel would always hold a special place in her heart for him, and as she delicately touched his portrait, she whispered "Thank you, Antonio." She finally felt at peace with everything and was ready to rest until she was needed at the atrium again.

Walking back into the palace, she was filled with happiness and strolled to her bedroom with a light heart. Once she had changed and slipped between the sheets, Azazel leaned back onto the thick, plush pillows beckoning sleep to come to her. She shut her eyes and waited for an eternity before she was lost in a dreamland, plummeting into one that was more of a memory, reunited with her sisters during a time of despair and turmoil.

The Earth had gone through a recent shift, and half of the

world was in a depression. Azazel and her sisters were sent to Earth to balance it; God thought that perhaps the three of them would be able to put everything back on the right track.

When they got to Earth, they saw how bad it indeed was. God had made it seem like it was going to be a simple task! Azazel saw starving children on the streets, crying out for their mothers who had abandoned them weeks ago in search of work and never returned.

There was so much pain in the world that the sisters came to the conclusion that God needed to intervene; He needed to save these poor sheep who cried out for Him in their prayers. When they returned to Heaven to tell Him that, He simply laughed and replied, "It's all part of my plan."

This angered Azazel. "How could making them suffer be part of your plan?!" she screamed in desperation. "You're supposed to be an all-loving God!" Her sisters had to hold her back as she crumbled with her belief in Him.

Her sisters held her as she wailed. The feeling of betrayal from her father left a dark stain on her soul, leaving her feeling empty and hopeless. When they were commanded to go back to Earth and guide the humans back to religion, prayer, and God, Azazel asked why they couldn't just help the humans develop new skills. Again, this caused God to laugh and spit at her, telling her that she was just an angel. She was created to do *His* bidding, not to think.

Her sisters pulled her away from God's presence gently, whispering that it would be okay, and they would find a way to help. Before they left Heaven, they vowed to support the humans anyway and every way they could, regardless of what God said.

Azazel woke up abruptly, her face drenched with tears and her heart pounding furiously; it felt so real. She looked down at her arm, and there was a red handprint where her sister had grabbed her. It was real; she knew it was!

Azazel looked around her room and called out, "Natalia? Raziel?"

She wasn't sure what to expect, but it wasn't just a dream. It certainly didn't feel like it! Once her breathing slowed down, she leaned back against the pillows again, wishing for dreamless and restful sleep. This time, she was back in Antonio's arms in their haven on the other side of the palace, happy, in love, and tucked away from the world. This was the Heaven that Azazel wanted to live in for eternity.

His kisses felt so soft on her skin, but when he looked up at her, his face was decaying, and his eyes were milky white, filled with death. Azazel woke up once more and screamed. She looked around and howled, "I will *not* feel bad about his death!"

She tried to force herself to stop her tears. Her mind went silent, but a small voice in the back of her head told her to just give in. Azazel looked around the room again in desperation. She was confused about what was happening to her and thought that maybe a bath would help her relax again. She pulled herself out of bed and walked into the bathroom. When she looked at herself in the mirror, she shrieked when she saw her reflection. She looked like she was dead! Her skin was loosely hanging on her frame, and her eyes were sunken in.

When Azazel lifted her shirt up, she counted every rib. When she looked up at her reflection, she heard, "I can make this all go away."

Azazel shook her head and replied, "Stop! You're not real!"

Her reflection said back to her, "I'm very real. I'm you." Then suddenly, the reflection's face started to morph into something that resembled a decaying body.

She took a step back and screamed in horror as the reflection continued, "I can make this all go away. I can make your pain—your guilt—all go away. All you have to do is give up control; no one will even notice a difference. Aren't you tired of feeling sad about Antonio?"

Azazel stared at herself and thought for a bit before asking, "You can take it away?"

The reflection nodded and replied, "You'll feel like you've slept for a hundred years and won't even remember him."

She didn't want to, but every part of her told her that she needed to give in; she needed to forget. She looked down at her decaying hands and whispered, "Okay."

Azazel screamed as she felt something frigid course through her veins; she felt herself falling, and everything went black.

25

Mulligan found Azazel on the floor. He noticed how thin and frail she looked, and he rushed over to help her stand up once she started to regain consciousness. When she looked up at him, he was taken back by how milky her eyes looked. Azazel seemed drowsy and out of it.

He helped her up and asked, "Goddess, are you alright?"

She snapped back, "Yes, Mulligan! Nothing you need to worry about."

He nodded and replied, "Right, I'm sorry, Goddess, but a full freezer is waiting for you at the atrium."

Azazel stood up and walked through the closet to go feast once more.

Mulligan had sent out a kingdom-wide announcement, stating that Azazel wasn't feeling like herself, and for everyone to avoid her at all costs. He knew that there would be at least two more after this feast before she would return to a state of peacefulness. She would surely have eaten her fill by then.

Her appearance and demeanor were starting to worry him; however, she had reached a new level of her hunger, and he wasn't sure what else he could do to satisfy her. He remembered tales passed down through his family about her; he knew what she was like when she first fell on Earth.

There were grand feasts weekly, and the population had significantly depleted because of her divine needs. No one knew what had happened, but one day, she became a softer version of herself and only requested sacrifices once a year. She called it the Cunning.

He knew that only a few families knew the truth; all of the elite families knew, and staff members who were generational workers at the palace knew what she indeed was. It still shocked him that Azazel had killed Antonio, though.

Mulligan became sad when he thought of all the people lost to Azazel's divinity; he thought of the young combatants who had only known how to train for a cause that no human could ever understand. As Mulligan reached the front of the palace and saw that Azazel was already coming back toward him, he asked if she'd had a good feast, and she nodded.

Before she walked past him completely, she said, "Mulligan, I want you to bring the tradesmen back. I noticed some chipped tiles in the basement chamber."

He stared at her and whispered, "All of them?"

"All of them."

He didn't say anything more as she left him standing in

the doorway. He watched as she walked slowly back to her personal chamber, and it looked like she was floating across the floor. He wasn't sure what to make of it, but Mulligan felt something shift in the kingdom for the worse, and he had no idea how to fix it. He knew what was in store for the tradesmen and was angry that he would have to lure them back here. It was already an incredible hassle to get them to keep their mouths shut after the first abduction. And Azazel thought they were going to come back quickly? Regardless of what he told her, each tradesman told him not to call them back unless it was an emergency, and Mulligan knew this would *not* be an emergency. He sighed and started to walk down the steps to go to the shops.

Azazel slowly walked back to her chamber. She could only think of having a bath. She felt the stench of death lingering around her, and she wanted to rid herself of it. She filled the tub with boiling water. Before letting it cool down even for a minute, she stepped into the tub. She lowered herself down into the depth of the liquid. The scalding water started to bubble around her.

Azazel leaned against the back of the tub and went over the meals that she had just devoured while also looking forward to meeting the substantial, burly tradesmen. They had gotten away from her before. But she promised herself that they would not be so lucky this time, and she would put her beautiful chamber to good use as a way of thanking them for their excellent craftsmanship. Azazel smiled; it was the least she could do after keeping them in the dark about the true purpose.

She hoped that Mulligan would hurry with this request; the hunger wasn't patient and would hold him responsible for every minute that it had to wait. She looked around the room and sighed. She figured it was time to get out of the bath and tend to her kingdom. She stood up, and as she stood up, she heard a knock on the door.

Azazel stepped out of the tub and wrapped herself in a large towel before walking out into her room. When she opened the door, Mulligan was standing in the hall, and he whispered, "Downstairs." Azazel smiled widely at him and walked out the door.

He asked, "Goddess, won't you dress first?"

She unraveled the towel from her body and dropped it to the floor, continuing through the halls naked, causing Mulligan to realize that she was far beyond his help. As she turned the corner, he whispered a prayer to a god whom he was sure had abandoned all who lived in the kingdom.

Azazel walked through the halls, oblivious to everyone's shocked reaction to her. When she reached the basement, she heard the men's screams coming from the chamber, and their fear filled the entire basement with a sweet scent that resembled bait. She walked toward the room, and as she opened the door, the screaming stopped, and the men all rushed toward the opening door in relief... just to pull back in fear when they realized who it was.

She slowly walked into the room and, in a low, raspy voice, said, "Gentlemen," which caused them to all push themselves to the far end of the room, all looking around and at each other. Like a lion stalking an innocent gazelle in the Serengeti, Azazel walked around the room's perimeter as they tried to move away from her.

She reached the part of the wall where the hidden shelves were, and she looked at the group of men to ask, "Besides the hidden shelves, is there anything else I should know about?"

Azazel pushed the wall in to reveal the weapons once more as they all shook their heads, and one of the burliest men in the group said, "Goddess, we did the work. Please, we have families!"

She looked at them with a devilish look as she asked, "What makes you think they aren't next?" As she picked up a large blade, the men all started to speak at once. Several rushed toward her before she held her hand up and stopped them in their tracks. The men behind them all stared in awe, and Azazel continued, "I am doing you all a favor by being naked and being the last beautiful woman that you'll ever get to see before you die, and all you can focus on is how you're locked in a room. You need to be grateful for the small things in your lives."

Azazel looked at the crowd, and a low growl came from the back of her throat as she lunged toward the group; the men all scattered, and one by one, she killed them, splattering their blood across the white tiles. The frozen men had no choice but to watch in horror as their partners were slaughtered violently.

Once the orbs started to float out of the bodies, Azazel went to the middle of the room and inhaled them all at once before turning to her last victims, who were all silently screaming and begging for salvation. Azazel walked toward them slowly, her naked body dripping blood, her hair completely saturated, making it look like she naturally had red locks of hair, and she had a psychotic, dead look in her eyes.

When she got closer to the men, she asked, "Do you know what I love the most?" When they didn't respond, she snickered and said, "Right, you can't talk. What I love the most is how much power human lives give me, how much beauty their blood gives me." As she started to circle them, she continued, "I was always powerful, but there's just something about a human's life source that puts my powers over the top."

She stabbed each man in the stomach and watched in glee as each one started to bleed out, but their screams were muted, and she walked around them again. "I also like how your sounds can be turned on and off." She watched as one man's eyes started to flutter shut, and she rushed over to help him collapse to the ground.

When she touched him, he was able to move again, but he groaned instead as he fell to the floor. Weakly, he reached for Azazel, who grabbed his hand—covered in blood—and started to lick his lifeblood off of his hand and fingers. He wheezed his last breath as she leaned down to start drinking the blood from the entry wound.

As she drank deeply from him, Azazel noticed his orb begin to poke through his lips. She smiled and let it float up toward ceiling to Heaven; she deemed him not worthy of spending an eternity with her for trying to attack her.

Azazel continued to drink the blood straight from the body until it stopped bleeding, and the body started to cave slightly from the pressure of her sucking blood through the gash. She looked up at the other men when she was done drinking and noticed that their eyes were shut. She stood up and pushed them over, making a loud thud. One by one, she watched as each orb floated up through the roof, away from her.

She knew she made the right choice when she went to drink more of one man's blood and recoiled in disgust when she tasted heavy nicotine and grease. Azazel stood up and looked at the bodies lying around her; she ran her hands up over her body, face, and through her hair, feeling like her entire body was on fire. She reveled in the delicious moment of finally achieving the prey she wanted, the prey that cost Antonio his life.

Azazel smiled when she thought of Antonio, remembering how scrumptious his last breath was. She started to walk to the door of the chamber, but was surprised when Mulligan opened it first. When he saw the crime scene that the chamber had become, his jaw dropped.

He looked at Azazel, and before he could say anything, she held a finger up and said, "It's your job, Mulligan. This room makes it as easy as possible for you." He looked back into the room, and she continued, "You should be thanking me for making your job easier, Mulligan. We have gone over how much I despise your ungrateful behavior."

He quietly thanked her and walked inside as she continued away from the scene. Azazel's nose was filled with the blood's sticky, coppery scent, and she wanted to bask in it for as long as possible. She turned toward the chamber, and when she saw Mulligan starting to clean up, she called out, "Drain four of the bodies and bring the blood up to my chamber, quickly!"

He stopped and looked at her. "Bring the blood up to you for what, Goddess?"

"I need to bathe, Mulligan. It's been a messy morning."

She didn't wait for him to respond; she left the room again, slightly skipping through the halls back to her chamber. As she was about to enter, she saw a young butler who was utterly shocked to see her in her bloody state. She requested that he bring her some tea. He bowed and tried to avoid looking directly at her before he turned to go back to the kitchen.

Azazel flung the doors open and walked into the room; she felt a renewed sense of happiness and optimism. She felt like her energy was finally starting to go back to normal. When there was a quiet knock on the door, she shouted for them to come in, and the young butler brought in a large tray with a delicate light blue tea set. He set it down, still averting her gaze.

She noticed and smiled as she started to walk closer to him and asked, "Does the female body make you feel uncomfortable?"

He quickly shook his head, but still refused to look at her. Azazel then got even closer to him, inspected his face, and said in a low voice, "You are incredibly handsome."

"Um, is there anything else I can do for you, Goddess?"

She smiled warmly and replied, "I made a bit of a mess behind the couch. Could you please help me clean it?"

When the butler walked around the couch and didn't see

a mess, he looked back at her and asked, "Where is the mess, Goddess?"

Azazel pointed toward the back. "It's a bit further; there was a bunch of glass just under the couch."

As he took a step forward, he triggered the trap door and dropped straight down the chute. The fallen angel giggled and yelled down, "Incoming, Mulligan!"

She heard the butler drop down to the chamber, and she quickly ran over to her bed, where she heard him screaming. Azazel didn't hear Mulligan, however, so she knew that would be a fun surprise for him later. As she enjoyed hearing the young man's screams, a knock sounded at her door, and she excitedly yelled for them to come in.

Mulligan struggled to get into the room with two large buckets before going back out to get more; she was excited to see him bring in six large buckets total. Azazel directed him to bring them into her bathroom and pour the liquid into the bathtub.

But he hesitated, and she glared at him. "Mulligan, pour the blood into the bathtub!"

He slowly began to move the buckets into the bathroom to complete his task. Once he was done, he came back out and said, "Goddess, it's ready."

When Azazel walked in, she saw that he had lit candles and even decorated the blood with flowers. "I always love when you go above and beyond for me, Mulligan." She stepped into the tub and shivered slightly before lowering herself into it. She sighed. "Mulligan, have you ever had something happen to you, and it just felt like it was the final piece of your life puzzle?" When he didn't reply, she continued, "Everyone who has been absorbed, there's been a reason for it. I keep all of you safe from the world outside of the kingdom's barrier."

Mulligan looked down and quietly whispered, "I'm sure

many people would rather deal with a harsh world than know that they could be selected for slaughter."

She shot daggers at him with her eyes. "Don't ever think you're above them for a second, Mulligan."

"Goddess, if you're going to kill me, do it already. I'm tired of holding the weight of your secret. I'm tired of scrubbing blood from my hands, just to see it again later."

Azazel stared at him and sarcastically said, "Mulligan, it's so gross seeing you beg. Get out of my sight!"

As she turned her attention back to her bath, Mulligan left as quickly as possible. As he closed the main chamber door behind him, he looked at his hands to see that they were shaking. He continued to walk away from the chamber and attempted to calm himself down.

Azazel cupped some blood with her hands and poured it over her head, enjoying the warm liquid streaming down her face and through her hair. She leaned back against the tub and giggled at Mulligan's newfound confidence to confront her like that. She had never thought of absorbing Mulligan before; he had become the clean-up crew, and she needed him. But if he was going to continue being an insufferable dolt about her needs, she would find someone new to take his position.

Once the liquid started to get cold, Azazel drained the tub and replaced it with fresh, clean water. She continued to wash until she was rid of all the blood, and when she was finished, she got out of the tub and went into the closet to pick out a dress for the final day of the Cunning.

She decided on a ruby red gown, and there were no jewels or grandeur to the dress. It was perfect and straightforward, and she paired the gown with a pair of strappy stiletto heels that had studs all over the straps. She changed, and when she looked at the mirror one final time, she was incredibly pleased with the look. Azazel quickly left the room and ran to the makeup room, where Dante had just finished spreading out all the makeup he needed.

"I need something quick, pretty, and simple," she demanded.

Dante quickly got to work. When he was done, he revealed that he had simply accentuated her beautiful skin and eyes with neutral colors, a bright red lip, and a long pair of eyelashes. He then finished her look with straightened hair. Azazel was pleased enough with it and thanked him before quickly taking off once more.

She had noticed how quiet he had been throughout the entire process. She had noticed that more people were avoiding her as she walked closer to them but paid them no further attention. Azazel had bigger—tastier—things to focus on.

The atrium soon came into view, and she started to quicken her pace the closer she got. The smell of death grew stronger as she neared the building. Azazel threw the arena doors open and continued to the freezer to absorb the latest victims before taking her place in the spectator's box to watch the final five fight to the death. She was pleased to see the forest landscape replaced with a giant gladiator-like fighting stage, and all of the combatants were being herded into the middle of the arena.

Azazel saw they were all beaten, bruised, and a few looked very close to death. A bell sounded, and they all began to engage in extreme hand-to-hand combat. She found herself excited when two were instantly killed from their injuries, slowing them down. The final three all started taking turns attacking each other. Finally, one of them fell to the ground and was stabbed in the throat before the other two continued fighting intensely.

The spectators watched as the stronger of the two executed a maneuver that his opponent couldn't block, knocking his rival to the ground, and stabbing him shortly after. Azazel stood up and began to applaud the winner, and was surprised when he dragged his blade across his own throat. She stopped celebrating and watched as masked figures ran into the arena to try and save him.

One of the family members looked up at Azazel and shook his head. She sneered and said out loud, "There is no winner this year!"

She was greeted by several family members when she stepped down to the arena, who all tried to explain what happened, but she held her hands up and said, "There is no problem here; this is actually the best-case scenario."

The family members stopped talking, and a man with a bear face mask asked, "Goddess, what do you mean?"

Azazel turned to him and explained, "I don't need to give money away, and since we have Antonio's funeral this afternoon, we can add a simple eulogy at the end." She grinned at everyone standing around her and asked, "Am I wrong?"

All of them rushed to reassure her and agree that it was a good decision, even though Azazel could feel an awkwardness in the air.

However, she silently dismissed it. "I am counting on all of you to help finish clearing the arena, and bring the families of the chosen up to the palace for the funeral afterwards."

She smiled at everyone while they nodded in agreement and dutiful acknowledgment. Azazel left the arena to go to the freezer and wait for the final combatants to be brought down. While she waited, she closed her eyes and basked in the moments before the final absorption. It crossed her mind that, maybe, this level of feasting didn't need to come to an end.

Azazel's thoughts were interrupted by several masked members dragging in the final combatants. When they dropped the bodies at her feet, a woman with a mask in the shape of a lion said, "Goddess, there are still several combatants in the freezer. We will bring these final warriors to you."

When she reached the freezer for the last time, Azazel decided that she would take her time and thoroughly enjoy each of these absorptions, and she did. She slowly bled each one out and whispered her appreciation to each sacrificed warrior before she absorbed their life force. She didn't even notice the final five combatants who were brought in until she was almost done going through the initial freezer stock.

Once she had consumed all of the combatants, she looked around the freezer and felt complete. She knew that this event was a success; Azazel felt unstoppable, powerful, and completely recharged. She left the freezer, pleased that no one was outside waiting for her.

She continued to walk to the palace through the empty atrium; the atmosphere felt different. As she got closer to the palace, she heard music and distant chatter. Azazel smiled and figured that people were starting to gather in the garden for Antonio's funeral, and now, the combatants'. She glided through the halls to her chamber to change into a black gown; she wanted to look the part of a mourning monarch.

When she went into her closet, she picked out a long black velvet gown with a deep V-neck and long tight sleeves, pairing it with a simple pair of pumps. Azazel was ready. She twirled one last time in front of the mirror and left the room. The halls were empty, but she could smell something delicious wafting through the hallways. She followed the smell until she was at the side door. Azazel let herself out into the garden, and when the kingdom citizens saw that she was approaching them, they all broke off to go sit down.

The fallen angel made her way down the aisle until she was in front of the crowd; they quieted down and waited for her to speak. Before she started her speech, Azazel took a deep breath.

"Thank you, everyone, for being here today to celebrate the life of Antonio Barem. He was truly something remarkable, and the kingdom will feel his loss for generations to come." She looked for his mother as she said this. Azazel wanted her to know that she meant it with her heart and continued, "I know that while his shoes will be big and hard to fill, that as a community, we can all come together and make it through."

There was a pause, and she heard sniffles throughout the crowd. Azazel didn't see Mulligan anywhere when she scanned the crowd and briefly wondered where he was. "We are also here to mourn our fallen warriors. There was no winner in this year's Cunning. There will be no prize distributed, but we will have a moment of silence for the combatants." She read out the complete list of warriors. Once the final name was announced, everyone bowed their heads in respect and went silent.

After a short while, Azazel raised her head and loudly announced, "Okay, that concludes this year's Cunning. To honor Antonio, we will be taking part in an extravagant feast that my head chef has so kindly catered to Antonio's taste buds." She beamed when she saw the servants bring out platters of food that looked absolutely decadent, and she watched as the kingdom started to funnel out of the garden to follow the food.

Azazel turned to look at the portrait of Antonio once more. This time, she pulled it off the easel and walked toward the palace with it. She wanted to hang the picture in her chamber for when she needed to see his reassuring face.

When she entered, she stopped. Her senses were in overdrive, and she sensed that something was off. Azazel slowly walked deeper into her chamber and looked around.

"Hello?!" she called out.

When there was no response, she continued to her closet and placed the painting on the floor. And as she looked in the bathroom, she saw that her blood bath residue had been thoroughly cleaned up. Azazel turned back out of the bathroom and still couldn't shake the feeling that something was off. She didn't hear any screaming when she stepped closer to her bed.

"Mulligan!"

When he didn't come instantly, Azazel stormed out of her room. Every servant she came across, she would angrily ask them if they had seen Mulligan anywhere. They all said they hadn't seen him for quite some time.

She stomped down toward the basement; the eerie

feeling followed her and intensified the closer she got to the chamber.

Azazel swung open the door, and she saw Mulligan sitting on a chair that she assumed he had dragged in with him. The butler was gone, and Azazel walked into the room and pointed around.

"You let another morsel free?" she asked casually.

Mulligan nodded and replied, "I'm tired, Goddess. I don't want to clean up your messes anymore; I'm tired of death."

Azazel laughed. "*I* say when you're done, Mulligan. Your family is nowhere near being done serving me."

Then she snapped her fingers. "Bring the butler back here now!"

But Mulligan stayed sitting down. He firmly replied, "I will no longer be doing your bidding, Azazel."

This caused Azazel to rush toward him, and she seethed into his ear. "That's 'Goddess' to you, every time you address me."

"You should just kill me for my insolence and constant insubordination, then."

She took a step back from him and asked, "You want to die that much?"

Mulligan nodded. "As long as I am away from you and your depraved version of reality."

"The life essence I absorb stays with me for eternity, Mulligan. You will never know true rest." He stared at her, and she asked, "Do you think your sacrifice will save the kingdom? Because it won't; it actually makes me want to start killing *more* people."

Mulligan's eyes widened. "Haven't you had enough? Haven't you killed enough people?

"It will *never* be enough. I could kill the entire kingdom and *still* be ravenous."

He shook his head. "Someone will stop you."

Azazel cackled. "Mulligan, I was banished from Heaven. *No one* is going to stop me. *No one* cares about this corner of the world, which is unfortunate for you and the rest of the meat suits outside of these walls."

He looked down at his hands and took a deep breath. "I pray every night that someone better, more powerful, and more deserving will come and kill you. Every night, I pray for that to happen."

She quickly rushed toward him and slashed across his neck with her nails, blood gushing violently. She got close to his ear as she whispered, "I am going to make sure you *never* find peace, you pathetic gutter rat."

As he gurgled next to her, she saw his orb push out of his lips, and she maneuvered it so it lowered to the floor. She stepped on it until it shattered and popped. Mulligan's body jumped as she squashed it, and Azazel grinned devilishly.

"I've decided to move in another direction. Your services are no longer needed."

She looked at the body and moved it with ease to where the chute leading to the incinerator was. Azazel shoved Mulligan's body into the chute and watched as it fell down into darkness and shut the door.

She chuckled. "Maybe I can be my own clean-up crew; there will be much less complaining." Azazel continued out of the chamber, and as she approached the Great Hall, where all the citizens were, she felt her hunger start to bubble. She smiled; it was feeding time, and perfect timing to pluck a plump chicken from her livestock.

She strolled through the halls with such force and power that the wind accumulated around her and started to slam every window and door shut as she passed by them. When she reached the Great Hall, the atmosphere was filled with love, and people were telling stories of their fallen combatants and of Antonio.

Azazel looked around the room, and she yelled loudly, "Dinner time!"

The entire kingdom turned to her and watched in horror as she morphed into her skeletal state. Azazel lunged at the people closest to her, snapping their necks violently; this caused hundreds of people to flee out of the nearest doors in fear. She captured as many people as she could, killing as many as possible. Half of the kingdom was lying lifeless on the floor; it looked like it had been repainted red. And Azazel was in the middle of it all, greedily drinking the gushing blood from a young woman's neck, when she heard a *whooshing* sound.

Azazel turned around and saw a vision. Two figures were manifesting in front of her, and as she saw their faces start to become more apparent, she hissed and growled a sound that resembled something from the abyss of Hell.

With blood pouring from her mouth and covering her body, Azazel lunged toward the figures as Raziel spoke authoritatively.

"Sister, your bloody tyranny is done. That's enough."

To be continued...

Viola Tempest is a dystopian fantasy and paranormal romance author who yearns to expose the truth of those in the modern world: the good, the bad, and the ugly. Her inspiration primarily stems from life experiences, those who annoy her, ex-boyfriends, and the crazy dreams that pop into her head every once in a while.